KEEPING HER

Book 1 of the Keep Me Series

ANGELA SNYDER

COPYRIGHT

Copyright © 2017 Angela Snyder

Cover Art ~ Addendum Designs

This book is a work of fiction. Names, characters, places and incidents either are products of the author's imagination or are used fictitiously.

All rights reserved. No part of this publication may be reproduced, stored in retrieval system, copied in any form or by any means, electronic, mechanical, photocopying, recording or otherwise transmitted without written permission from the publisher. You must not circulate this book in any format.

This book is licensed for your personal enjoyment only. This book may not be resold or given away to other people. If you would like to share this book with another person, please purchase an additional copy for each recipient. If you're reading this book and did not purchase it, or it was not purchased for your use only, then please return to the retailer and purchase your own copy. Thank you for respecting the hard work of this author.

ISBN: 1974512509
ISBN-13: 978-1974512508

AUTHOR'S NOTE

Keeping Her is Book 1 in the Keep Me Series and is not intended to be read as a standalone.

The books in this series feature adult content and touch upon some very serious issues and sensitive topics that could be considered as triggers for some readers.

You can find all of my books exclusively on Amazon and free for Kindle Unlimited subscribers: http://amazon.com/author/angelasnyder

And please sign up for my newsletter to be notified of all of my new releases, giveaways, sneak peeks, freebies and more: http://eepurl.com/cNF0o5

KEEPING HER

(KEEP ME SERIES BOOK 1)

"She calls to me like one of the Sirens from Greek mythology, and I would gladly crash into a thousand jagged rocks for just a single touch from her."

To say I had a rough start in life would be the understatement of the century.

My uncle may have rescued me from my abusive childhood, but he couldn't save me from the neurotic and compulsive obsessions I would develop in my adulthood.

I deal with some of the worst criminals in the seedy underbelly of the world just to get what I want. What I need.

And what I need is the perfect woman. Perfect and pure in every way possible. And I'm willing to obtain that perfection...no matter the cost.

So when I make my newest purchase, I expect Adeline's fate to be like all the others before her --- taking what I want and then never seeing her again.

But she's different.

Her beauty is disarming.

And even though I promised to let her go after I took what I wanted...I slowly come to the realization that I can't.

I have to break my promise to her, because she's mine now.

And I'm keeping her.

PLAYLIST

Falling in Reverse - *Coming Home*

Palisades - *Let Down*

Highly Suspect - *My Name is Human*

The Plot in You - *Feel Nothing*

Breaking Benjamin - *Breath*

Hellyeah - *Love Falls*

Lana Del Rey - *Love*

Denmark + Winter - *Every Breath You Take*

ACKNOWLEDGMENTS

Thank you, first and foremost, to my friends, family, and especially my husband, for understanding my need to get lost in the books I'm writing, even if it means ignoring everything and everyone around me in the real world for a while.

A huge thanks to Ashley W. Sometimes I just don't know what I would do without you and your advice. Thanks for always telling me to "let it go".

To my eagle-eyed beta readers: Ana Rita C., Brandy F., Courtney J., Lawanda J., Lisa T., Melisa G., Rachel Lyn A.B., Robyn B., and Sandra E.K. Thank you for your time, encouragement and support.

TABLE OF CONTENTS

PROLOGUE 1
CHAPTER 1 9
CHAPTER 2 13
CHAPTER 3 19
CHAPTER 4 23
CHAPTER 5 29
CHAPTER 6 33
CHAPTER 7 38
CHAPTER 8 43
CHAPTER 9 49
CHAPTER 10 52
CHAPTER 11 59
CHAPTER 12 69
CHAPTER 13 72
CHAPTER 14 79
CHAPTER 15 82
CHAPTER 16 87
CHAPTER 17 91
CHAPTER 18 95
CHAPTER 19 109
CHAPTER 20 114

CHAPTER 21 118

CHAPTER 22 123

CHAPTER 23 138

CHAPTER 24 143

CHAPTER 25 152

CHAPTER 26 155

CHAPTER 27 160

CHAPTER 28 164

CHAPTER 29 170

CHAPTER 30 174

CHAPTER 31 180

CHAPTER 32 182

CHAPTER 33 186

ABOUT THE AUTHOR 192

PROLOGUE

GIOVANNI

I AM DESPERATE.

In all honesty, I'm beyond desperate at this point. I have a deadline that I'm supposed to meet, but I don't have the goods to deliver to my client.

And as I look over at my fiancée sleeping peacefully on the couch in my living room, the sinister idea that I've had for weeks now strikes me again. *Hard.*

Shaking my head, I force the thought out of my skull immediately, but it only takes a few moments before it comes right back again.

My eyes stray to the sleepin' beauty. Thick, dark lashes sweep across her rosy cheeks, her normally porcelain skin turned a ruddy shade of pink from spending too much time on the beach with me today. Her long, chocolate brown locks cascade over the armrest of the leather couch in soft waves, and her small hands are curled under her cheek.

She looks picture perfect, and that's because she is…in every way.

Even though our imminent marriage is an arranged one and orchestrated by her father and my boss, Salvatore Valenti, I like to think that I would have chosen Adeline under normal circumstances, not only for her beauty on the outside, but for her beautiful, kind soul. She's breathtaking beyond belief both inside and out.

However, bein' forced to do something has always made me fight that much harder for the complete opposite. So, when Sal thrust this marriage proposition in my face, let's just say I wasn't pleased.

Salvatore's late wife bore seven children, all of them girls. Adeline was the last one to be born shortly before her death, and so Valenti never received what he really wanted --- a boy. An heir. Someone to carry on the family business and the family name.

Sal didn't get a son, but one of his daughters could still bear an heir for him. With four of Adeline's sisters dead and the other two married to schmucks that Sal never approved of and would never welcome into the family, Adeline is the only one unmarried…and not dead.

So, with his choices limited, Salvatore chose me, one of his most trusted employees, someone he took under his wing from an early age, to take on the task of marrying his youngest and producing an heir.

Being that Adeline was Sal's only option left, I think that's why he locked her up from a young age. Why she was homeschooled; never allowed to venture out in the world.

And that's also part of the reason why I eventually conceded to Sal's marriage proposal between Adeline and me. I felt sorry for her, knowing what she'd been through as a child, knowing how lonely and broken she was.

It's not Adeline's fault that we're getting married, though, so I try to not show any anger towards her. She's as much the innocent bystander as I am at this point, although I have much more to gain than she does.

Sighing deeply, I turn my attention back to the computer and close my eyes, pinching the bridge of my nose and trying to ward off the migraine that is hitting me full force. I read over my client's email again as my hands clench into fists against my thighs. I wouldn't even be in this situation right now if it wasn't for Adeline's father.

Unfortunately, I have a reputation to uphold, and the drug trade is too damn crowded for me to make as much money as Salvatore requires. He takes such a huge cut of my profits that I have to make five times as much to please him and to keep my lavish lifestyle.

I'm useful to Salvatore at the moment. And now that I'm his future son-in-law, he's been requiring much more of me. And I *cannot* disappoint him. I've seen what happens to guys who disappoint the all-mighty Valenti mafia king, and it ain't pretty.

Shuddering at the thought, I think back to when I first made the decision to deal in the flesh trade. It was a recommended alternative by a mentor of mine with a promise to be extremely lucrative. What can I say? There are a bunch of pervs out there that are willing to pay almost anything to have the kind of girl they want. And the most profitable girls on the market are *virgins*. You can get sometimes double or triple the amount of money for them, but they're about as easy to find as a fuckin' unicorn. I guess that's why men pay top dollar for 'em.

Salvatore doesn't care how you make the money that pads his fat wallet and keeps him in business. In fact, he doesn't even want to know. He just wants a significant portion of whatever his hired men make, not caring how people got hurt or had to die in order to get it.

That man has no fuckin' conscience.

If I go through with this transaction, things will never be the same between Adeline and me. But it's only one small dark spot in what could be a lifetime of happiness. And I will do my best to make her happy. I will go above and beyond to make her forget all about the darkness she is going to endure because of me.

My fingers tremble against the keys as I type out the email to my client. I only know him by his alias--- *The Big Bad Wolf*. I don't know his real name, and I know his IP address is fake since it's always pinging at crowded cities throughout the world and never the same location from day to day. He covers his tracks well, and that's why halfway through the email I stop typing and hesitate.

I've been dealing with The Wolf for a while now. This will be my fifth transaction with him. The first four girls weren't easy to find, but it was worth all the trouble when he paid me handsomely for them. If a supplier can't meet his demand, The Wolf, along with my other clients, will move on to find someone else to satisfy their needs. And I desperately want to keep him as one of my buyers, because he's a solid guarantee for a lot of fuckin' cash for me.

From what I understand and from the rumors I've heard from another seller that has dealt with this particular buyer is that The Wolf releases the girls soon after he takes their virginity. He never keeps them long after the girls give him what he purchased them for in the first place. And then he's quickly on the prowl, looking for another girl to meet his demands.

The fact that he lets the girls go after he's finished with them is what gives me a sense of optimism for what I'm about to do. Salvatore Valenti is leaving his empire in New York City to visit an affiliated mafia clan in California for a few weeks. It's perfect timing.

Almost too perfect.

And if everything goes according to my plan, Salvatore will not even know his daughter is gone, and she'll be back before he returns to New York, none the wiser. Then, I'll convince Adeline to not tell her father about what happened, assuring her that it will only upset him and get me in trouble. I'm sure it won't take much convincing considering she does everything she can to keep her father happy.

And then, after this whole nightmare is over, I'll help her get through whatever happened to her while she was with The Wolf.

Once more I glance at my beautiful fiancée. Her crimson lips move as she mumbles in her sleep, and I can't help but grin. She's pure. Innocent. Not allowing me to sleep with her until after we're married. That's more of her father's rule I think, but she follows it to a T.

It's a shame that I haven't even had a chance to sample her. I wanted to be the one to take her virginity on our wedding night, and it pains me to think that I won't be her first. If I go through with this, I'll be her second…but also her last.

My eyes dart to the email message, and I force myself to keep typing. I have no other choice at this point. My money is slowly dwindling, and I need a flush of cash fast.

Big Bad Wolf,

I have what you want, but it's going to cost you. One-hundred percent pure, virgin, 5'4", around 125 pounds, beautiful with dark hair, as you requested.

You will receive the goods once I receive the cash.

And I expect her to be released once you get what you paid for.

Signed,

Supplier

I encrypt the email and send it through a series of undetectable servers. The man on the other side of this message should be receiving it soon.

Feeling sick to my stomach, I back away from the computer and stand up. Pulling out my cell phone, I dial a number I have memorized but rarely use.

When his deep, gravelly voice answers with *hello*, I tell him, "I need your help with something." I hesitate before I say the next words. "I need to make it look real. I need it to be believable. I'll text you the details."

Unable to steady my nerves after ending the call, I go to the fridge and crack open a beer. Taking a long swig, I make my way back to the living room where my Adeline is still sleeping soundly. She has no idea how much her life is about to change.

I feel shitty for being the one responsible for the pain and heartache she's about to endure, but there's no other way around it. My customers have needs, and I supply the girls for those needs…no matter what. I didn't make my millions by having a heart. In fact, if it weren't beating out of my chest right now on adrenaline, I would think that all that resided in my chest was an empty, black hole.

My lips seal around the bottle's edge as I pour more alcohol down my throat. I'm gonna need a shit ton more alcohol if I'm actually going to go through with this.

I sit on the large leather couch beside the girl of my dreams. Her eyebrows crease, and her full lips part as she mumbles incoherently. She's having a nightmare I realize. *How fitting*, I think to myself, *considering I've been planning her real-life nightmare for the past hour.*

Hushing her, I work my fingers through her beautiful hair and down her cheek, soothing her out of the bad dream. Her murmurs stop, and her face finally relaxes from my touch.

Leaning down, I kiss her soft, full lips, allowing myself to linger there for a few seconds. Then I lean back, studying every inch of her gorgeous face. I just sealed her fate with that kiss. In more ways than one.

A pounding at my front door awakens my sleeping beauty. She moans softly and stretches, flashing me a timid smile that has my heart skipping a beat. Adeline is the most beautiful girl I've ever seen, and I still can't believe her father chose me to be her future husband.

I've watched her grow up from a shy girl and blossom into a beautiful, young woman. It was weird at first, trying not to picture her as Valenti's daughter but a possible mate for life. But it's not like I had much choice in the matter. Valenti does what he wants, and what he says goes.

The pounding starts again, and I grumble as I stand up, setting my empty beer bottle on the coffee table. "Stay here," I tell her.

When you work for the Italian mob, you never know who may be at your door. But when I glance at the clock on the way to the entrance of my condo, I have a good feeling as to exactly who it is.

"Fuck," I curse under my breath when I check the security cam on the small video panel. Salvatore Valenti, the devil himself, and four bodyguards are stationed outside my door.

Steeling myself, I unlock and open the door and am met with a pair of black, beady eyes belonging to my boss and future father-in-law.

"Where's my daughter?" he hisses through clenched teeth. Before I can answer, he pushes past me to storm through the entrance of my condo. Adeline must have known what was coming, because she's already up and off the couch, smoothing her skirt as she plasters on a saccharine smile for her father. I can see right through her, though. She's fucking terrified. *Just as I probably should be.*

"Do you have any idea what time it is?" he snaps at her.

Her eyes instantly move to the floor. She twists the engagement ring, which I placed on her finger just four short weeks ago, around her finger nervously. "No, Papa," she whispers demurely. "I fell asleep on the ---"

Without warning, Salvatore grabs his daughter by the hair and yanks her towards him. I cringe at the action, but it's not like I'm not used to it by now. I've seen him manhandle all of his daughters, but it always seems like he saves most of his anger for his youngest, Adeline.

Sal treats his daughters like dolls, wanting them to be perfectly poised and bending at his every whim, but he has no qualms about roughing them up and putting them in their place.

I'd open my mouth, but I would be signing my own death warrant.

You can't ever tell Sal he's wrong...unless you enjoy swimming with concrete blocks tied to your ankles, that is.

Trying to placate the situation, I approach them carefully and explain by saying, "We had a long day at the beach. She fell asleep on the couch, and I lost track of time going over paperwork on my computer."

Salvatore's attention snaps to mine, and he narrows his eyes. "If you touched her..."

I hold my hands up defensively. "I would never," I tell him honestly, and I fuckin' mean it. "I want to keep my head," I say with a smirk, attempting to crack a joke, but Salvatore is in no laughing mood.

"Nothing happened, Papa," Adeline says quickly, and I can hear the tremor in her voice. "I swear. I swear on Mama's grave," she whispers, her lower lip trembling as she holds back tears.

Salvatore stares at her face, studying her, perhaps trying to see if she's lying. Then he releases his tight grip on Adeline's hair and pushes her to the floor. She falls on all fours and stays down like the good little doll he raised her to be.

He turns to me and holds up a stubby finger. Salvatore is about as wide as he is tall with a huge paunch he carries around with the swagger of a much taller and thinner man. "No more mistakes, Giovanni. My daughter is not some *toy* to be played with," he barks.

I almost laugh out loud considering he treats her exactly as such, keeping her up on a shelf and not allowing anyone to look and touch as if she's a prized vintage toy still in the original wrapping.

Schooling my features, I nod and tell him, "It won't happen again. You have my word."

Sal grabs Adeline by the arm and hauls her up, his grip no doubt leaving bruises. "I'll deal with you when I get home," he threatens in a low murmur. Then he pushes her towards his awaiting bodyguards, who escort her out the door.

Salvatore motions for them to leave, so they do, but he decides to stay. He's not done with me yet. We both know I fucked up, and we both know what must happen because of it.

"Honestly, Sal, she fell asleep and ---."

But I don't get to finish my sentence before he socks me right in the jaw. I remain standing, though, not giving a fuck whether the stocky Italian before me keeps hitting me. I refuse to fall at his feet like a coward.

But the second hit never comes. Instead, Sal curls his fat fist in anger and says, "You only have a few months until the wedding. I suggest you keep your dick in your pants until then. I won't have my daughter being a fucking harlot, not fit to wear white when she walks down the aisle."

"Like I said, Sal…it was innocent."

He eyes me once more before nodding in satisfaction. "Good, good," he says, standing up straighter and fixing his suit, which got rumpled in the process of him showing everyone who's the boss around here…as if anyone could forget. "I'll see you tomorrow before I leave for Cali."

"Sure thing, Sal," I tell him, wiping the blood from my busted lip and giving him a final nod.

I watch the older man leave, and then I lock the door behind him. I'm already second-guessing my decision to sell Adeline to The Big Bad Wolf, but the deal is already done. If all goes according to plan, Salvatore will have no idea what I did, and we'll both be richer after the whole ordeal is over. Adeline will be back in her gilded cage before her father even knew she was missing, and I'll be able to sleep a hell of a lot easier at night knowing I have the funds to keep myself and my boss happy.

Still, the nagging feeling in my gut doesn't leave me as I toss and turn that night in bed. In the stillness of the night with only the sounds of my heartbeat to keep me company, I think I finally come to terms with what I've done to Adeline, the woman who is to be my wife.

I fed her right to *the wolf*.

And I just may regret that decision for the rest of my life.

CHAPTER 1

LUCIEN

I AWAKE FROM a nightmare, jolting straight up in bed, drenched in sweat. After struggling out of the maze of tangled sheets, I swing my legs over the side of the mattress. Running my hands through my damp hair, I draw in deep, urgent breaths as I try to forget the visceral assault on my senses that just occurred.

It's the smell that stays with me the longest. It's as if the overwhelming stench of cigarettes, booze, chemicals and cat piss somehow seeped into my lungs, drowning me in my sleep.

Memories of my horrible childhood come to me almost every night in the form of petrifying, vivid nightmares. And no matter what I do, peaceful sleep always seems to escape me.

Standing, I make my way to the en-suite bathroom, ready to begin my day even though the clock on the nightstand reads that it's three in the morning. As I walk, my body is coiled with tension, and I just can't seem to shake the nightmare.

My childhood was something you'd likely hear about on the local news station. I could be one of those people that they invite on daytime talk shows to discuss their horrible pasts and how much suffering they endured as a child. Hell, I'd have enough material for a two-part episode, keeping the audience riveted to their seats and crying in pity.

But my past was never discovered by talk show hosts or police officers or case workers, for that matter. I knew from a young age that no one was coming to rescue me or save me from my retched life like in all those godforsaken fairytales I read as a young boy.

No. I had to suffer and endure as best I could until the age of twelve...when everything suddenly changed.

My savior came in the form of my uncle, my mother's brother, whom I had never met before that day. William visited our single-wide trailer in the middle of the blistering hot summer to tell his sister that their father, my grandfather, had passed.

I never knew my grandparents. My mother ran away from home when she was seventeen after getting hooked on heroin. Her family never heard from her again, and no one ever knew I even existed. She got knocked up with me at the age of eighteen and never sought the help she most certainly should have from her parents.

And so after the death of their father several years after their mother, my uncle decided to hire a private investigator to find his long-lost baby sister.

Imagine the shock on William's face when he saw me, a twelve-year-old boy covered in his own filth and weighing as much as a kid half his age.

William saw me that day. He actually saw me...instead of looking right through me like I didn't exist and like I had grown accustomed to over the years.

And then he saved me. Ripped me out of the clutches of that horrible life and brought me into his world.

And what a world it was.

My uncle was rich. Beyond rich. And he had things I only ever dreamed of, but never knew existed.

However, I knew from the moment I stepped foot into the 12,000-square-foot mansion that I didn't belong there...and probably never would.

I refused to sleep in the king-sized bed that smelled like fresh linen, and instead opted for the closet, never wanting to become too comfortable or letting my guard down.

I snuck food constantly, so afraid that my next meal would never come and that I would once again feel the excruciating hunger that I used to feel when I was a boy.

I think at that point I was waiting for the proverbial rug to be pulled out from under me at any given instant.

And so I waited…and waited…and waited, but my uncle never sent me away. No matter how many times I acted out and no matter how many times I disappointed him.

Eventually, I began to accept my uncle's help and kindness, along with that of his son's. Jackson, my newly acquired cousin, was the same age as me, but we couldn't have been more opposite. The biggest difference being that Jackson was…normal. And I was anything but.

I was able to become a chameleon of sorts, however, hiding my obsessive compulsions and blending in to the point of normalcy. It took a lot of practice, but in time, people began to regard me with looks of respect instead of expressions of pity.

Nothing came easy to me back then or even now, but I wouldn't want it any other way. Every single accomplishment is another *fuck you* to the nasty whore who brought me into this world.

And as I glance at my reflection in the bathroom, I regard the man staring back at me in the mirror. The scared little boy I once was is gone now, hidden deep down in the dark recesses of my mind.

My dark eyes are bloodshot from lack of sleep, and my chestnut hair is a complete wreck from running my hands through it a few moments ago.

Letting out a frustrated growl, I turn the water in the shower on as hot as I can stand it before stripping out of my clothes and stepping into the spray.

Once the scalding hot water cascades down my body, I instantly begin to feel better. Lathering up my hands with an antibacterial soap that smells masculine and clean, I scrub my body for over an hour.

Showering is like a ritual for me. When I'm in this glass-enclosed safe haven, nothing seems to bother me, and I can just simply focus on the task at hand. It's a very short reprieve in my day from my fucked-up thoughts and neurotic impulses.

After my very long shower, I dry off, style my hair into a perfect coif and iron my shirt and pants before getting dressed. While I'm buttoning the cuffs of my dress shirt, my phone alerts me to a new email. It's the email I've been waiting for for weeks now.

A wicked smirk appears on my face as I stare at my reflection in the mirror.

My day just got a whole hell of a lot better.

CHAPTER 2

ADELINE

"YOU'RE NOT CONCENTRATING, Adeline."

The voice of my piano teacher makes me jump, and my fingers stumble over the keys, creating a horrible combination of notes and making him cringe in disgust.

"I'm sorry, Mr. Moreau," I tell the tall, lanky man hovering over me. He's older, in his sixties, and he's trained some of the world's best pianists. When he retired to New York City several years ago, my father hired him to give me lessons; thus, replacing old Mrs. Beaumont, who started teaching me at the tender age of five.

To say Mr. Moreau is tough to please would be the understatement of the year.

He watches my every move as I continue with the Chopin composition, his narrowed eyes still projecting his disappointment over my blunder.

He's absolutely right about me not concentrating, and I inevitably stumble over the keys once more, much to his dismay as well as mine.

"Stop," he says before sighing exasperatedly and grumbling under his breath as he reaches into his brown, leather bag on a nearby chair. He retrieves a metronome and places it on top of the piano. That's something I haven't had to use since I first learned to play when I was a little girl, when I was starting to learn the harder pieces of music.

He's clearly trying to embarrass and undermine me.

And it's working.

I shift on the hard bench seat and cringe from the shooting pain that rockets up my spine. My back and bottom are covered in bruises from the beating my father gave me when we got home. He used his belt on me the moment we stepped through the front door. I thought when I got up this morning that there would be blood soaking my sheets from the severity of the beating; but, fortunately, he didn't break the skin…this time. I'm just severely bruised from my collarbone to my thighs.

More bruises to add to the ever-growing collection on my body, I think to myself. It's not the first time my father has beat me for some minor infraction, and it certainly won't be the last.

The piano teacher sets the metronome to a steady pace and says, "Begin again." And then he adds, "And *try* to keep the timing this time, *Adeline.*" He says my name as if it leaves a bitter taste in his mouth.

The rhythmic clicking threatens to drive me up the wall, but I take a deep breath, letting it out slowly. And then I begin the Chopin piece again, keeping in perfect timing just like he asked.

And that's something I always strive for --- to be perfect. *Always.*

My whole entire life I have had people around me always demanding perfection --- my father, my teachers, my tutors, my dance instructors, my father's associates and so on. And I'm always quick not to disappoint and be the epitome of a perfect Italian mafia princess…so that I don't have to endure the consequences of attempting to be *average.*

A knock at the door startles me out of my thoughts and breaks my concentration. I end up making a few sour notes on the piano before stopping altogether in frustration and balling my hands into fists on my lap. Mr. Moreau scowls at me and stops the metronome before going to answer the door.

One of my father's guards peers inside and tells me, "Piano lesson's over. Your father's gettin' ready to leave, and he wants to say goodbye to you before he goes."

I have to force myself not to roll my eyes. My father doesn't want to tell me goodbye. He wants to tell me not to mess up while he's gone. He wants to enforce his rules, ingrain them inside of my head until I can no longer think about anything else.

But what he doesn't understand is that he's already done that. He's been doing that my whole life.

Last night was a mistake. A careless mistake. I have a curfew, albeit a new one since I was never really allowed to leave the house before my father deemed Giovanni Morello a suitable future husband for me.

Gio and I have been on three dates. *Only three.* And after a long day on the beach yesterday, I foolishly fell asleep on his couch.

I'm sure normal twenty-somethings get in a whole hell of a lot more trouble than that, but they have the good fortune of not being under my father's rule.

In a strange way, the beating was worth it, though, because it meant for at least one night I was actually *living* outside of this home, which is more like a prison to me.

Sometimes I think that I'm nothing more than a living, breathing porcelain doll to my father. He takes me from my shelf to show off to his friends, but then I'm returned to the same spot when he's done with me.

I'm forced to stay in this house under supervision, under lock and key almost twenty-four-seven. My father tells me it's for my own good because of who he is and how many enemies he has, but I'm starting to not believe that any more. I'm not the naïve little girl he raised by himself after my mother died shortly after I was born.

And the more he lets me out of the house to be with Gio, the more I start realizing that my life is anything but *normal*, like I once believed it was.

I bite back any hateful words that want to spit out my mouth and follow the guard downstairs, grateful to at least escape my torturous piano lesson. My father and his entourage are all standing in the giant foyer of the mansion, and all eyes connect with me as I glide down the stairs in seamless form.

I'm wearing a long, dark gray dress with simple heels, and my hair is styled flawlessly off to the side on one shoulder. I did my makeup a little darker and heavier today in an attempt to hide my swollen eyes from the crying jags I had last night and this morning.

People tell me I'm beautiful all the time, but my father beat the self-confidence right out of me years ago. I'm never good enough for him no matter how hard I try, and I'm made to constantly feel like I'm failing him.

And so I always look my best, no matter the occasion, and don a mask of flawlessness in the hopes that one day it will be enough.

I just want to be enough.

My father stands proudly, wearing a dark, pinstripe suit, red tie and his signature fedora, looking very much like the mob boss that he is. When he glances at one of his goons, who looks like he wants to eat me alive and is literally starting to drool, he smacks him in the back of his head and mutters, "That's my daughter you're looking at."

Immediately, all the eyes in the room focus on something else other than me…all of them except one pair of hazel eyes that I never want to stop staring.

Giovanni is leaning against the wall in a casual dark suit sans tie and with a blank look on his face. When he sees me glance in his direction, though, a crooked grin instantly graces his mouth. And that's when I notice the bruise on his jaw and his cracked lip at the corner. I realize that must have been the punishment he received from my father last night. And it's all my fault. I'm the one who fell asleep on his couch instead of going home in time to meet curfew, but Gio received part of the blame.

Feeling completely mortified, I stare down at the floor, no longer able to face my future husband.

My father holds his arms outstretched, and I reluctantly go to him. He crushes me to his chest in a hug, pressing against my bruised back, and I bite my lip to keep from crying out in pain. Tears well in my eyes, and I gently sigh with relief when he finally lets me go.

My father stares into my eyes and wipes a stray tear away from my cheek. "I'll be back before you know it, Adeline," he tells me, obviously convinced I'm crying because I'm going to miss him.

I glance at Gio, who is giving me an empathetic look. I wonder if he knows… It wouldn't surprise me if my father bragged to him about my beating. My father loves to brag about all the horrible stuff he does to me to "put me in my place"…even when he thinks I'm not listening.

Giovanni steps forward. "Sal, would it be all right to take Adeline to dinner tonight?" he asks suddenly.

I hold my breath as I wait for the answer. My father will no doubt be angry about the request considering what just happened last night. I wait for him to make a decision, and he takes his time glancing from Gio to me and then back again.

"That's fine, but I'm sending Bruno and Dario with you. And don't even think about bringing her back here after her curfew this time, Giovanni," he warns.

Gio nods in compliance and then winks at me once my father's back is turned. I can't help but smile. He certainly has become the only light in my dark, lonely world as of late.

We watch my father and his men leave, and then it's just Giovanni, me and some other of my father's hired help milling about the mansion.

Gio gently places a hand on my shoulder. "Did your father hurt you last night?" he asks in a low voice so no one else can hear.

"Not any more than he usually does," I admit fretfully.

Giovanni winces at my words. Then he takes my hand and pulls me into the study, closing the door behind us. "Adeline," he starts, but then pauses, his eyes searching the floor as if he's trying to find what he wants to say. When his hazel eyes meet mine, he says, "I know I may have seemed...reluctant when your father first arranged this relationship between us."

Reluctant is a poor way of putting it. I remember when my father first tried selling him on the idea of marrying his youngest daughter, producing an heir and, consequently, taking over the family business. All three of us were in my father's study, and Giovanni had angrily slammed his fists on the desk, causing me to jump. He outright refused my father's proposal, saying he was too old for me and that he could never see me as anything more than a little girl.

Giovanni is twelve years older than me, but I never saw our age difference as being an issue once I turned eighteen. And now that I'm twenty-one, I think the disparity in our ages is insignificant.

Gio takes my hands in his, pulling me out of my reverie. "It's only because I watched you grow up. I just couldn't think of you like that. But now…now I've come to realize how beautiful you are inside and out. And I want you to know that I'll always protect you."

I stare up at him with adoration. He has no idea how much love I have for him already. I've had a crush on Giovanni ever since my father first took him under his wing. He's always been a handsome and powerful man, and his presence constantly took my breath away when he entered a room.

In fact, it still does.

"If anything ever happens to you, know that I'll find you. I'll always be with you…in here," Giovanni says with a very serious look before pressing his fingers against my chest right over my heart.

My heartbeat stutters under his touch, and he flashes me a breathtaking smile that has me practically melting to the floor.

"I have to go now, but I'll pick you up for dinner at seven," he tells me before placing a quick kiss on my cheek and leaving.

It takes me a few moments to gather my wits before I go upstairs to get ready for our date tonight.

CHAPTER 3

LUCIEN

WHILE THE ENCRYPTED email is running through a special decryption program, I think about what it might contain.

My interaction with this particular supplier has been a difficult but rewarding one. Even though he's always right under the deadline date, he manages to somehow pull through with exactly what I need.

He has supplied me with the last four girls that have been to my home. The first two were from a different supplier, who now seemed unable to fulfill my requests.

I give the handlers a specific set time to comply with my demand. If they fail, then they don't receive one red cent from me. But if they succeed…then they're paid handsomely for delivering exactly what I want.

An alert pops up on my large computer screen, notifying me to the fact that the email has been decrypted and is ready to read.

Taking a deep, steadying breath, I close my eyes for a moment before clicking open the message.

Big Bad Wolf,

I have what you want, but it's going to cost you. One-hundred percent pure, virgin, 5'4", around 125 pounds, beautiful with dark hair, as you requested.

You will receive the goods once I receive the cash.

And I expect her to be released once you get what you paid for.

Signed,

Supplier

My eyes rake over the words again and again until my vision blurs. Squeezing my eyes shut, a rare smile graces my lips.

This will be the seventh girl that I have purchased to fulfill my obsession.

Lucky number seven.

The number has great significance to me. It was July 7th, 1997 when my uncle rescued me from the hell formerly known as my childhood.

Perhaps this will finally be the one to end my sick obsession, I think to myself.

I've been trying for years to get over this fascination I have with purity and control. So far I've been unsuccessful in finding a cure….if one even exists.

My fixation with cleanliness, order and control started soon after my uncle found me. It started off small with not wanting to eat off dishes or drink from glasses that someone else had used before me even though they had been thoroughly washed. That somehow manifested to wanting perfection in every possible thing around me…including people.

The thought of being with someone who had slept with other people sickened me. I needed someone pure, someone unblemished.

Unfortunately, it's been hard for me to find such women over the years. And that is precisely what led me to my latest supplier, Giovanni Morello. I pay him large sums of money to find exactly what I desire the most.

Now, putting my fate into the hands of corrupt people is not ideal, to say the least, but I have an uncontrollable need that must be met…no matter the cost.

I buy these girls, most of them stuck in a world they don't want to be in, filled with filth and abuse, not much unlike my own past, and I turn them into the perfect specimen right before I take one of the most valued assets they have to offer --- *their virginity.*

And even though it makes me feel full of shame that I'm, in a sense, helping the supply and demand aspect of human trafficking, the girls I take are all willing. In a way I feel as though I'm actually their savior, rescuing them from a much more horrible fate than what I could ever produce.

After I'm done sleeping with a girl once, I send her on her way with a large sum of cash and a new identity, if she so chooses. Then she's able to live the rest of her life in luxury.

All they have to do is give me one time with them --- their first time. That's all I want. And then I send them off into the world with more money than they could probably spend in a lifetime. I know they receive a small cut from their handlers, but I would imagine it doesn't amount to much, if they even get paid at all. It definitely wouldn't surprise me to learn that the handlers, who are from the seediest underground in the world, are dishonest to the girls I buy.

Unbeknownst to any of the girls that I've purchased in the past, I check on them periodically. All six girls that have left my home are living the life they always wanted but could have never had before they met me. And I suppose in that way, I feel like their knight in shining armor. They just don't realize it while they're here how much of a savior I am to them. No, that realization comes much later...after they leave this place...after they receive their money.

I like to think that this seventh girl, who meets my specifications to a T, is going to be the girl that ends it all for me. Maybe once I have her, I'll finally be satisfied.

I can only hope that is the case.

Lucky number seven.

My eyes flit over the message even though I have it memorized.

And then I do something I haven't done in any of my transactions in the past. I request a picture of Number Seven from my supplier.

My hands tingle in anticipation as I type out the email, encrypt it and send it off into the dark web.

He's never been able to find me a girl that met my specific stipulations, and I'm anxious to put a face to the description he gave me.

I just hope I'm not disappointed...for her sake.

CHAPTER 4

ADELINE

GIOVANNI TAKES MY hand in his and leads me out of the trendy and romantic Michelin-starred restaurant in downtown New York we just dined in. It was one of the fanciest restaurants I've ever been in, and the food was to die for. I'm feeling a little tipsy from the expensive bottle of wine we shared, and I stumble in my heels in the doorway before Gio catches me in his strong arms with a chuckle.

"Careful," he says before bringing my hand up to his mouth and placing a gentle kiss on my skin. I bite my lip and smile as I stare up at him. As we leave the ritzy place, I feel like the luckiest girl in the world when I'm in his arms, as if I'm walking on a cloud.

Giovanni's dressed in a tailored three-piece suit, and I'm wearing the sexiest little black dress I own with the highest pair of heels I can manage to walk in. When Gio picked me up earlier, he told me I looked stunning, and I should hope so considering it took me all day to get ready. I wanted to look perfect for him.

And if the way he can't keep his eyes off of me all night is any indication, I'd say I achieved my goal.

Once we're on the public sidewalk, Giovanni turns to me and says, "I'm glad your father agreed to let me take you out again so soon after what happened last night..." he says, his voice trailing off.

I grimace inwardly. I was mortified by my father's actions, but it's not like I'm not used to them. I glance up at Gio and gently brush my fingertips over the bruise on his jaw and the cut on his lip. "I'm sorry for ---" I start to tell him, but he silences me by pressing his lips against mine.

His hands cup my face as he holds me in place, his tongue running over the seam of my mouth. I open up for him, allowing his tongue to tangle with mine. He tastes like the wine we just shared, and I can't stop the whimper that escapes my throat.

My stomach feels like a million butterflies are inside, fluttering their wings all at the same time. This is only our fourth date since becoming engaged. We haven't done anything but kiss and hold hands, but I want to do more, so much more. I want Gio to be my first...for everything.

I've been kept under lock and key for so long that even a night out like tonight feels like a dream, like I'm watching myself on a movie or something. I want to experience the world with Gio by my side, and I know that's what he wants too. Even if he doesn't say the words. I can see and feel the hunger in his eyes that he has for me.

Giovanni breaks our connection by taking a step back before giving me a small smile. I know exactly what he's thinking. My father would kill him if he ever found out we did anything before our wedding. And that thought alone keeps us both unwilling to cross any lines with one another.

"Let's take a walk through the park across the street," Gio suggests, surprising me. "I'll have Bruno and Dario take the car back to my condo, so we can be alone for a bit."

I stare up at him like he's grown a third head. After what just happened last night, I didn't think Gio would want to bend the rules so soon. Maybe it's because my father is out of town and so he doesn't fear the consequences of his actions.

"Really?" I squeak. We never leave anywhere without the accompaniment of my two bodyguards, and my father would most certainly forbid it. My father is a very powerful man, and so the need for constant protection for me is a must. Feeling uneasy, but not wanting to displease him, I nod and say, "Sure. A walk sounds nice."

Giovanni turns to the bodyguards waiting at the black town car just a few feet away. "We're going to walk, boys. You can take the car back to my condo. We'll meet you there."

Bruno and Dario exchange a look before Bruno asks, "You sure, Mr. Morello? I don't think the boss would like that very much." Bruno is the bigger of the two, but they both look like professional wrestlers with bulging muscles packed tightly in matching, black Armani suits.

"It's only a few blocks," Giovanni assures them with a calm, but demanding voice that sends a shiver up my spine. "Besides, the boss is in Cali for the next few weeks. He won't even know."

The two bodyguards eventually concede and reluctantly get in the car and disappear into the night.

Giovanni stares down at me and smiles. "Alone at last," he says with a chuckle.

I intertwine my fingers with Giovanni's and look up at him with adoration. In a way, Gio is my own personal savior. He's going to be plucking me from a life of solitude and anguish. I never feel those two things when I'm with Gio.

It's not like I don't have a good life at home. I do. I know I'm lucky in a lot of ways, and I know it could be a lot worse, but sometimes I just wish I had more…freedom. And I wish my father didn't demand perfection from me every second of the day, punishing me for every minor transgression.

I shudder at the thought of my beating last night, and Giovanni wraps an arm around me as we cross the street. "Cold?" he asks.

I shake my head and just smile up at him as we start walking through the park. I never walked through here at night or without the accompaniment of bodyguards, but Gio makes me feel safe no matter where we are. Gently, he tugs on my shoulder, bringing me in closer to him as we walk.

Even though my father chose Giovanni as a husband for me, I feel like we're a compatible match. He's handsome with dark hair, tall and muscular and has a great sense of humor. He can be very serious and distant at times, but I like to think that he could one day grow to love me as his wife.

Giovanni has been under my father's tutelage for a while now, rising to the top of the ranks quickly. And when I turned twenty last year, my father made a decision --- he wanted me to marry and eventually have an heir to take over the family business. My mother never had any boys, just seven girls with me being the youngest. She died shortly after child birth, and so my father's chance of having an heir seemed to solely rest on my shoulders, unfortunately.

He chose Giovanni to be the man to carry on the family name and run the family business. He trusts Gio, and that cannot be said about the husbands of my other sisters.

I can't say that I'm disappointed in who he's chosen even though I secretly wish I could have found love myself. But when you're the daughter of the biggest Italian mafia boss on the east coast, you don't get to have choices. I learned that from the moment I learned how to talk.

We walk and walk until my feet begin to ache in my high heels. Gio leads me from the park, across the street and down what appears to be an alley. When we come out the other side of the alleyway, I glance at our surroundings and realize I have no idea where we are. There is barely a soul in sight, and the businesses on this side of the city are all dark and abandoned.

This isn't the way to his condo, I think to myself. "I think we went the wrong way," I tell him, nervousness edging my tone. I twist my engagement ring with the large solitaire diamond around my finger. It's a nervous habit I've picked up as of late.

Giovanni seems distracted, and so it takes him almost a full minute before he realizes I said something. "Oh, must have taken the wrong street," he mumbles. Then he glances up at the street signs, studying the names.

My brows crease in confusion. Giovanni should know these streets by heart. He grew up in NYC, after all. But I don't question him. Instead, I tell him, "Let's just walk back the way we came. I'm sure if you called Bruno ---."

Suddenly, Giovanni stops walking and pulls me towards him. He leans down and kisses me so hard, so passionately that my knees go week. When he pulls back, there is an indescribable emotion etched on his face. I'm about to ask him what's wrong when I hear a clicking sound behind us.

It takes me a long moment to realize what's happening.

"Give me your money, and no one gets hurt," says a deep and

terrifying voice.

I turn to see the gun aimed right at my heart, and I shudder in fear. "Giovanni," I whisper in a trembling voice.

A man not much taller than me, but much bigger in width, stands a few feet away. He's dressed in black with a ski mask over his face. I glance past him and see at least two more men all in black waiting nearby in the shadows.

Giovanni's grasp on me tightens for a moment before he releases me and whispers, "It's all right, Adeline." He puts his hands up defensively and turns his attention to the gunman. "Hey, man, you don't have to do this. Just turn and walk the other way, and we'll forget this even happened."

The men walk out of the shadows towards us while the gunman takes a step closer to me. There were more than two lurking in the dark. My head spins as I realize there are four men now standing behind the gunman. We'll never be able to fight all of them off.

"Give me your money, bitch," the leader hisses, waving his gun at me to emphasize his point.

I glance down at my dress and realize I left my purse in the car with the bodyguards. The streetlamp above us lights my diamond ring up like a beacon, and I quickly pull the ring off my finger. My father bought it for Giovanni to give to me, so I have no qualms about giving it to this man in exchange for saving our lives.

The gunman steps forward. And just when I think he's going to snatch the ring in my outstretched fingers and take off, he grabs my hand and yanks my back against his chest, pushing the gun hard against my temple. My ring slips out of my grasp and bounces on the dirty street before disappearing into a muddy puddle.

"Please!" Giovanni begs the man. "Let her go!" He pulls out his wallet and starts throwing hundreds on the ground as if they're worth nothing. "You want money? I have money."

"I want more than money," the man replies, and an icy chill freezes the blood in my veins.

All of a sudden, my fight or flee sense kicks into high gear…and so I begin to fight. I squirm against the man's hold, throwing back my elbows and kicking him hard in the shins. A whoosh of air escapes him with a bitter curse when one of my elbows lands in his stomach.

Regaining his control of me quickly, the man's hold on me tightens to the point that he constricts my breathing. Struggling for air, the last word I hear him spit out is "bitch" before he slams the butt of the gun against my temple.

I hear Giovanni calling my name, but it sounds like he's far away…and under water. Suddenly, I'm doused in a sea of darkness, drowning in it and not knowing if I'll ever resurface again.

CHAPTER 5

LUCIEN

THE ANTICIPATION OF their arrival is the hardest thing to deal with, especially with *Number Seven*.

Jackson, my cousin and most trusted friend --- hell, my *only* friend, will be flying the girl in today. Judging from the radar on my computer screen, they should be arriving within the next hour.

Minimizing the tracking screen, I bring up the email from my supplier for probably the fiftieth time today.

My eyes flit over the message even though I have it memorized.

I have what you want, but it's going to cost you. One-hundred percent pure, virgin, 5'4", around 125 pounds, beautiful with dark hair, as you requested.

Virgins are the most valuable in the flesh trade. I should know. I pay top dollar for the ones I buy. But I know I need to eventually stop all of this and do the right thing. And the right thing is bringing down Salvatore Valenti's empire and all the men under him, including my current supplier, Giovanni Morello. Then, when the mafia empire crumbles for good, I'd be saving all the girls, not just some of them like I have been doing.

I pull a stack of bright green post-it notes and place it in front of me. My hand trembles as I grip a black marker and write the words *Eliminate*

Salvatore Valenti and Giovanni Morello.

I tear off the note and stick it to the edge of my computer desk, along with dozens of other notes of things that I want to do or need to do after I rid myself of this sick obsession of buying women to fulfill some overwhelming need inside of me.

I've tried everything over the years to find some sort of miracle cure for my transgressions --- medication, hypnotherapy, psychological testing --- and nothing worked.

As one psychiatrist put it one time while he stormed out of his very own office, "I'm too fucked up to cure."

Never were truer words spoken.

My childhood did a number on me mentally, and I don't think I'll ever truly be cured. In all honesty, I agree with the numerous therapists on one thing --- my unconventional behaviors are the only way my brain can block out all of the horrible things that happened to me and allow me to function as a semi-normal adult. If I somehow find a cure and rid myself of these obsessions, I'm afraid of what will happen to me.

Feeling even more anxious than before, I place the unused stack of notes back in their proper place and return my attention to my computer.

It's almost time.

My eyes focus on the email string between Morello and me once again.

When my supplier told me he found the exact type of girl I wanted, I demanded a picture, something I've never done before. In the past I liked to be surprised besides knowing their measurements, so that I can order accurate clothing sizes. But I always preferred to see their face for the first time in person. It heightened my anticipation and hunger.

But with this girl, *Number Seven*...I wanted --- no, I *needed* to see her as soon as possible.

It took Morello almost eight hours before he responded to my request, and I honestly thought the anticipation would kill me.

When I pull up the picture he attached to the email for what feels like the thousandth time today, I suppress a moan in the back of my throat. He finally found me exactly what I wanted --- a dark-haired beauty with light green eyes. All the girls in the past haven't been to my specifications, but my suppliers tried. Oh, they've all tried.

I request brunettes with light eyes because I want the exact opposite of my mother. I don't want to be reminded of her in any way, shape or form. All the girls in the past have been blondes. Not the particular shade of dirty blonde my mother was, thankfully.

I study the girl's picture closely and can't help but feel a sense of apprehension. She looks…happy. So much unlike the other girls in the past, although I never asked for a picture to be sent before.

The others had been poor, needing and craving the money and luxuries I gave them.

This girl is on the beach, her long tanned legs stretched out before her on the sand. Her long, dark hair cascades around her shoulders in soft waves, and she's smiling a flawless smile with straight, white teeth.

She doesn't look like someone I would expect to need money. In fact, she looks like the exact opposite.

My thumb brushes against her full, glossy lips, and then I curse as I realize I probably left a smudge on my screen with my carelessness. Quickly, I reach into the top drawer and bring out a cleaner and wipes. I spend several minutes cleaning my computer screen, making sure my thumbprint is gone, before I put everything away and stare at her beautiful face once more.

Maybe I'm reading too much into the picture. It's not like I saw her predecessors in their before state. Perhaps this was just one great day out of her usually miserable life. Yes, that must be it.

I can't help but wonder what condition she'll be in when she gets here. All six of the previous girls have come in here dirty and damaged, roughed up by their handlers, against my wishes, of course. But I have to admit that part of the fun for me was returning them to pristine condition before I took what I paid for.

I need complete and utter perfection before I lay a finger on them.

And I won't settle for anything less when this girl comes under my ownership…even if her beauty most likely will disarm me.

No.

She will be exactly what I crave and precisely what I need.

She will be absolutely *perfect*.

CHAPTER 6

ADELINE

I WAKE UP slowly, my head throbbing with a tremendous pounding that feels like someone knocking on the side of my temple with a hammer. Groaning, it takes me a few times to be able to sit up. It takes even longer until I'm able to open my eyes. And when I do, I just want to close them again.

I don't know where I am.

The room is dark except for the moonlight shining through two skylights in the ceiling. The realization that I'm lying in someone else's bed in a strange room hits me hard. I press my fingertips to the pounding on my head and feel crusted blood matted with my knotted hair.

What happened to me?

I think back to the last thing I can remember, and the horrible flashes of memory come back to me all at once. Giovanni and I were on a date. We left the restaurant. We were walking…we were lost…and then a group of men tried to rob us…the gunman grabbed me…and then I must have blacked out. I'm trying to remember what happened after that, but I'm drawing a blank.

The harder I try to think, the more pronounced the fierce pounding becomes. I cry out in pain and grip the sides of my head.

When the pounding settles to a dull ache, I decide to find out where I am. Did Giovanni save me from the gunman and take me to a friend's house or something to recover? That's the only plausible thing I can come up with at this moment.

Pulling back the blankets, I realize that I'm no longer wearing the little black dress that I had spent hours picking out before our date. I'm wearing some type of thin cotton gown with no underwear under it. Who the hell undressed me?

Panic starts to rise in my chest as flashbacks of sensations begin to bombard my overwhelmed mind. I remember someone poking me with a needle and the sense of feeling like I was flying and falling.

I fumble in the almost pitch-black room and manage to find a table beside the bed. My fingers land on a solid object, and I squint in the darkness trying to figure out what I'm touching. When I realize it's a small lamp, I search for a switch, finding one after what feels like forever.

Holding my arms under the dim light, I search for evidence of my flashbacks. There is some bruising and definite needle marks on the inside of my elbow. *Did I have an IV…or was some kind of drug injected into my veins?*

Slowly, I crawl out of the bed on unsteady legs, gripping the mattress to keep my balance. My legs feel heavy as if I've been sedated with something. That coupled with the fact that I have a lot of memory loss makes me thinks that someone must have drugged me.

But *why?*

And *who?*

I slowly manage to make my way to the door. Holding myself up against the wall, I reach for the handle. It takes me a few fumbling tries before I'm able to focus and find it with my fingers. I pull the latch and pull, but the door is stuck. With all of my strength that I'm able to muster, I yank on the handle, cursing when it doesn't open.

I search for a lock of some kind, but find none. But through my inspection, my fingertips come upon a new discovery. Some type of keypad beside the door. My blood chills as I stumble back and fall on my ass to the floor. *I'm locked in here.* "What the ---?"

"You can only enter and exit with the code," a dark voice says from behind me.

Screaming, I scramble to my knees and search the dark room for the source of the voice. "W-w-who are y-you?" I stammer, my entire body shivering in sheer terror.

Out of the corner of my eye, a tall, dark figure rises from a chair in the corner of the room. "My name is Lucien."

My mind scrambles to find some memory of his name. Does he work for my father? Is he an enemy of my father? I search and search, but come up empty. I've never heard the name Lucien muttered before. "W-where am I?" I ask the dark shadow.

"My home," he answers simply.

This must be some sort of mistake that I'm here. I can't remember what happened after Giovanni and I were mugged, but this is all wrong. I'm not supposed to be here. Shaking my head, I crawl back to the opposite corner of the room near the bed and press my back against the wall. I'm panting, completely and utterly exhausted and feeling like I just ran a marathon. My entire body feels lethargic; my limbs heavy from what can only be some sort of sedative.

"Did you...did you drug me?" I ask breathlessly.

He doesn't answer right away. "Your handler should have told you that it would be necessary for your trip here."

Handler? My trip here? The thought of not being in New York City anymore and under the protection of Gio and my father has me folding in on myself, hugging my knees to my chest. I've never left the city, let alone the state before. "Where am I?" I ask him again.

"You already asked me that, and I already answered you." His tone suggests he's bored, impatient even.

I frown at his answer. He damn well knows I want a location more precise than his home, but I know I'm not going to get any more information. "Why am I here?"

A dark chuckle comes out of the shadows. "Enough of the twenty questions. This isn't how this works." After a deep sigh, he then says, "Your handler should have explained everything to you."

This isn't how what *works?*

He mentions my handler again as if I should understand what the hell he's talking about. I could ask him a thousand questions, and it still wouldn't tell me everything I desperately want to know. Instead of uttering another word, I decide to remain quiet, hoping that he will tell me more.

He takes a few steps out of the shadows, and the moonlight cascading through the skylights highlights his face. I notice his dark hair and dark, piercing eyes first. Then I study his statuesque and handsome features. He's clean-shaven and dressed in an impeccably tailored dark suit and tie. He doesn't look like a kidnapper or someone who would keep a woman against her will.

But I guess looks can be deceiving.

"You're here because I'm the one who bought you," he says, answering my earlier question and bringing my worst possible fear to fruition.

When I was a little girl, a few of my sisters were kidnapped and held captive by enemies of my father. My oldest sister, Isabella, was sent back home…one piece at a time.

A violent shudder rips through me at the idea that I'll probably have the same fate as Isabella, and I watch as a smirk forms on the man's face at my reaction.

"My father will pay you whatever ransom you're asking for," I blurt out before I can stop myself. My father doesn't negotiate with kidnappers or enemies. He always told me it makes him look weak. That's why four of my sisters are dead and only three of us, the three that managed to never be kidnapped, still have a pulse.

He quirks a brow and cocks his head to one side at my statement, but remains silent. His dark eyes narrow and watch me intently, studying me as the only sound in the deafening silence of the room is my panicked, rapid breaths.

After what feels like an eternity, he finally tells me, "You can clean up in the bathroom." He motions over his shoulder to an adjacent room. "Someone will bring you breakfast soon."

Before I can say anything else, he's stalking to the door, inputting a code that I can't see, and leaving. The door closes behind his retreating form, a beep and a click signaling that I'm locked in here.

KEEPING HER: BOOK 1 OF THE KEEP ME SERIES

CHAPTER 7

ADELINE

HE JUST LEFT. I wait with baited breath, thinking that he'll return.

But he never does.

My breathing becomes more erratic as my anxiety spikes to a new high. A sob rips through my throat as I struggle to stand and make my way across the room to the adjoining bathroom. I close the door, pressing my back against it. Flicking on the ceiling light, I turn and search for a lock on the door, but there isn't one. Desperate, I stare around the room. There's a bathtub and shower combo with glass doors, toilet and a cabinet with a built-in sink. I swing open the cabinet doors, hoping for something I can use as a weapon. There are towels, toilet paper and other bathroom necessities, but nothing that will prove to be helpful in my situation.

Feeling frustrated, I lean against the sink and let out a painful moan. My entire body feels sore like I was hit by a Mack truck, and then the truck backed up and ran over me again. My head is pounding with the worst headache I've ever felt in my life, and my legs feel like they're being weighted down with lead bars.

A large rectangular mirror is above the sink, and I slowly meet my reflection in it. I gasp at the sight before me, not believing that's it really me that I'm seeing. I'm covered in blood and dirt and god knows what else.

Black streaks of mascara stain my cheeks as if I'd been crying for hours. *Maybe I was*, I think to myself.

My hand shakes violently as I bring my fingertips up to my temple where blood is caked and matted into my tangled hair. When I touch the wound, I hiss and cry out in pain.

I back away from the mirror, no longer able to face the pure, undiluted fear present in my eyes. Staring down at the stained nightdress I'm wearing, I cry out in frustration and rip it over my head. I ball it up in my hands angrily and throw it in the corner of the room. I fold my arms across my breasts and run my hands up and down my scraped and dirty arms, barely keeping it together. I'm on the verge of hyperventilating as I drag ragged breaths in and out of my lungs.

I can't remember the past however many hours of my life. I don't know who has had their hands on me, where I've been, what happened to me or where I am now. I've never felt so dirty and scared in my entire life.

With the sudden urge to feel clean, I walk to the shower and run the water until it's the perfect temperature. I rummage under the sink and snatch a few clean, fluffy towels. I set them on the sink before I step into the shower under the spray of water.

I groan in ecstasy at the feeling of the water cascading down my body. I put my hands against the wall and face away from the spray, letting the warmth hit my back. I stay like that for a long time, relishing in the comfort.

When I glance up, I notice that there is a shower caddy filled with an assortment of shampoos, conditioners, body washes and soaps. I grab one of the shampoos and pour a large amount into the palm of my hand before returning it to the caddy. It smells like coconut as I suds my hair up and scrub vigorously, being careful of the sore spot on the side of my head.

I rinse and repeat two more times. Then I set out to wash the rest of myself, using half a bottle of the peach-smelling body wash before I finally feel clean.

The desperation of my situation slowly begins to set in, and I wonder how the hell I'll ever escape from this man --- Lucien, as he calls himself. Tears stream down my face and mix in with the water as I sob under the stream of water.

I have no idea where I am or why I'm here. When I mentioned my father paying a ransom, he didn't give me any inclination that he's interested in money. If he doesn't want money, then he must want something else.

Me.

The thought of being raped and it being my first time completely guts me, and I sob even harder. I slap my hands against the tile, screaming out in agony.

Why is this happening to me? What did I do to deserve this?

And then I remember that my sisters never deserved what happened to them either. When you grow up in the Italian mob, bad things are expected to happen. My father explained that to me from a young age.

He molded me into the perfect daughter, but apparently that wasn't enough to keep me safe. If only Giovanni wouldn't have wanted to walk home…

Giovanni.

A beam of light in this dark situation suddenly shines through. Giovanni would have seen who took me, and he would have told my father. Maybe they're working together right now and trying to track me down.

But then a more sinister thought creeps into my mind…what if Giovanni is dead? What if the man kidnapped me and killed him?

Fresh tears surface and stream down my face as I cry for what feels like forever. If Giovanni is dead, then all hope for anyone to come save me is gone. No one will know where I am, and I'll be stuck here…maybe forever…or until this man --- *Lucien* --- wants to kill me.

It isn't until the water starts to run cold that I finally get out of the shower.

I dry off, wrapping a dry towel around my long hair and tying it on top of my head in a sort of turban. Realizing I don't have anything to change into, I bite my lower lip and think about my options. I don't know who could be in my room. What if Lucien came back? Or what if it's someone else?

He told me that he's the one who bought me, but are there more monsters lurking out there like him?

I stare at the door. It's not locked. In all reality, they could have come in if they really wanted to.

Strumming up some courage, I yank the door open and peer out. The room is silent…empty. Slowly, I creep out of the bathroom, my feet sinking into the plush carpet as I walk.

Sunlight streams through the two skylights high up in the ceiling, but I can only see fluffy, white clouds in the bright blue sky. There aren't any other windows in this room, and that thought depresses me even further. I at least wanted to see some familiar surroundings, to know that my father might be closer than I originally thought and that I could be going home soon.

The aroma of food hits me, and my stomach growls right on cue. On the bed is a lap tray with a covered dish and two cups filled with what looks like water and orange juice. As I approach the four poster king-sized bed I take notice that the bed was meticulously made while I was in the shower, and it smells as if the sheets and comforter have been freshly laundered.

I wonder if Lucien made the bed and changed the sheets or if he has staff here. The prospect of other people being here lifts my spirits. Maybe if I explain my situation, they would help me.

Needing to get out of this towel and into clothes, I turn around and search the room for a dresser or something that would contain clothes for me to change into. The only furniture in the room is the bed, a small table with a lamp and a few occasional chairs in the corners.

When I turn back to the bathroom, that's when I notice another door to the right. It looks like it might be a closet, and so I go to it, hoping for the best. I turn the handle and pull the door open. A light instantly flickers on above me, illuminating a walk-in closet filled with racks and racks of clothes, mostly dresses, and shelves filled with shoes.

I pull open some of the drawers under the shelves and am happy to see underwear, although it looks more like lingerie. I rummage through the thongs and underwear and pull out a lacey pair of black panties. I read the tag and am amazed that it's my size. Curious, I pull out another pair and then another and then another, reading the tags as I go. Sure enough, they're all the same.

Feeling a sense of panic, I begin to hunt through the dresses hanging above. Tag after tag after tag all show size seven.

My exact size.

It's as if everything was all planned for me to come here. I slowly come to the realization that this is so much more than a kidnapping for ransom, and it might not even involve my father at all. I was kidnapped for a different reason entirely.

The blood in my veins turns to ice as my fears are confirmed.

Lucien is planning to keep me here…for a while.

CHAPTER 8

LUCIEN

I SIT IN front of the computer in my office still feeling apprehensive from the turn of events that have taken place since my newest purchase arrived three days ago. Number Seven had seemed to not understand where she was or why she was here. Now, granted, she looked like she had a nasty bump to the head, which Jackson had noted might have resulted in a concussion and loss of consciousness. Also, she was drugged, as they all are, before being brought here. But her confusion and the terror I saw in her eyes still have me perplexed, because it all seemed so *real*.

And when I'd mentioned her handler, her expression told me nothing but pure and utter bewilderment. Does she truly not know why she's here and what I want from her, or is this simply all an act?

It wouldn't be the first time a girl tried to change her mind.

But I can't remember ever wanting one so much that I desperately didn't want her to.

Sighing, my eyes flit to the wide computer screen in front of me that is currently displaying multi-camera angles of Seven's quarters. Before I even brought the first girl in, I had cameras installed in that specific bedroom. Like watching a science experiment, I study their reactions, their moods, the way they talk and act when I'm there versus when I'm not. Every girl has behaved in the same manner, had the same responses and actions. It's almost like it's the same girl every time, just a different name.

For the most part, their initial reaction is to get in the shower, at my suggestion, and then get dressed and wait. They sleep and eat and interact with the staff and wait for me to return, to explain what's going to happen and when it's going to happen.

I do not communicate with the women after the initial introduction for a period of three days. It's not because I want them to go crazy with anticipation or worry. On the contrary, I would love to take what I paid for on the first night and send them on their way. But there is the matter of tests that must be done. Every girl is subject to a thorough screening for drugs, STDs and communicable diseases before I will ever lay a finger on them.

Jackson draws blood from the women the moment they arrive on my property. And then it takes him three days to take the tests to a private lab and come back to me with the results.

And so, during my three-day wait, I sit back and bide my time by watching my purchases, studying them and thinking about the moment I'm going to take what's mine.

All of my prior experiences have been exactly the same, and I've come to expect every single reaction…except for now.

As I watched Seven that first night, I noticed small idiosyncrasies and differences between her and the others. The time she spent in the shower was mesmerizing and hypnotic, the way she washed her hair and body over and over and over, getting as clean as possible.

Her predecessors showered, but they never took any special or extra care in doing so. They were in there for twenty minutes tops.

Number Seven showered for exactly two hours and forty-seven minutes, and I was glued to the monitor for the entire time, hardly blinking and not able to tear myself away from the image of her perfect body.

And knowing how clean she was when she emerged from the bathroom made me want to rush in there and take her at that very moment. Fuck my rules, fuck the test results.

I fucking wanted her.

Consequently, I have spent the past three days agonizing and locking myself in my office so that I wouldn't go to her. I've never wanted any of the other women as much as I want this girl. I like to think that having a picture of her ahead of time caused a buildup of almost excruciating anticipation, but I don't know if that's truly the real reason.

She's different. I can sense it already.

When Jackson finally returned with the blood test results this morning, I felt relieved but also anxious. Even when he assured me everything was normal, I still read the tests over and over again, memorizing every word.

And as I look down now to read over the results for what must be the fifteenth time today, a small grin forms on my face. She passed. With flying colors. And I couldn't be happier. I didn't want to have the misfortune of ending up with someone tainted again, and I shudder at the memory of how I had to send a few girls home soon after they arrived because they didn't pass my tests.

I notice movement on the smaller window on my screen, and I see Jackson punching in the code to my office, a code that only he and I are privy to. All of my electronic equipment, the phone system, files and documents are kept in this room, and I make sure they are kept safe and secure at all times.

He swings open the door with a smile on his face. That's the thing about Jax. He's always in a good mood it seems, always finding the silver lining in everything. He's a lot like his father in that aspect.

My uncle was a great man, and I miss him dearly. That man saved my life, but I could not save him from the cancer that ate away at his body until he was nothing but an empty shell of his former self.

Even at my uncle's funeral, Jax was cracking jokes and telling stories about his old man, making everyone laugh amidst all the tears from losing such a kind-hearted soul.

I wish I could share the same blue-bird-on-my-shoulder-shitting-fucking-rainbows attitude. But, of course, I have more of a doom-and-gloom sort of temperament.

"You're *still* looking at the test results?" Jackson asks, but there is no real curiosity in his tone. He knows my rituals and has, reluctantly, become accustomed to them.

I give him a simple nod and look up at him. He reminds me so much of his late father, my uncle, since they both share the same dark hair and warm, steel-gray eyes.

I don't remember my biological father, and I've only seen one picture of him decades ago when I was a small boy. We shared the same dark hair also, but I don't remember if we resembled each other in any other way. However, who knows if my mother was even telling the truth about the man in the photo.

She liked to lie…about everything.

"How is she doing?" Jackson asks, and his sudden interest in one of my girls is unusual. Usually he just goes about his business, helping me here and there with bringing them to me and sending them away. Other than that, he minds his own business.

I think that's why we get along so well.

"I haven't been in her room since the first night. You know my rules," I tell him.

He sighs and plops down into a leather chair not far from me. "I do. And I also know that you're keeping tabs on her from your little camera feed you have on your comp." His fingers pick at the stitching on the arms of the chair, and it drives me up the wall. When he notices my obvious discomfort, he instantly stops. "Sorry," he says with a smirk.

My eyes narrow as I glare at my cousin. "Why the sudden interest, Jax?"

He shakes his head and leans forward in his chair. "It's not what you think. I just wanted to make sure that bump on her head didn't give her a concussion or anything." He rests his elbows on his knees. "Was she acting strange when she woke up?"

I hesitate. *Strange?* Perhaps. But it's not like I even know the girl.

Jackson can sense my apprehension, however. "What's wrong?"

"She seemed…confused."

He considers that for a moment. "That could be a sign of a concussion. What was she confused about exactly?"

"Everything," I confess.

Jackson stands suddenly. "Maybe I should go in there and talk to her. Maybe I could ---."

"No," I snap, suddenly feeling very protective and...jealous over this girl I barely know. "I will talk to her tonight. At dinner. I will find out how she's feeling and if she's aware of her situation."

He sighs, knowing that he won't be able to change my mind. "Fine. I'll probably be hanging out in the kitchen. If anything happens during dinner, come get me. I can check her vitals and everything in the matter of a few minutes, make sure she's okay."

"I will."

"And see if you can find anything out about the bruises on her body. There were some fresh and some old. Someone's been hurting her...for a while," he says, his eyes turning dark.

I'm taken aback by his sudden protectiveness over her. A part of me wants to scream out to him that *she's mine*. But I stop myself from telling him that. Instead, I agree by giving him a simple nod.

I watch as Jackson leaves, and then my gaze locks on my computer screen once more. The girl's still lying on the bed, staring up at the ceiling and inadvertently right at the undetectable camera concealed in the ceiling fan. Tears stream down her pretty face, and I watch her full lips open on a sob.

She's been crying almost the entire time she's been here. And while normally I wouldn't give a shit or even think twice about it, for some reason, with this girl, I feel...strangely guilty about keeping her here.

I think back to what Jackson told me about the bruises covering her back. And even though I shouldn't care about what happened to her before she got here, I can't stop from wondering...and worrying. Who was hurting her?

Shaking my head to clear my thoughts, I tell myself it doesn't matter. And it certainly doesn't matter how Number Seven's reacting or how different she is. After I get what I paid for, she'll disappear just like those before her, and I'll never see her again.

Perhaps she's second-guessing her decision for coming here, and that is what is making her so upset. But one thing is for certain --- she's here because she said yes to my request from her handler, Giovanni Morello. If she's regretting her choice now, she needs to realize that it's too late. The deal is done, and she has to keep up with her end of the bargain that I paid so generously for.

Tonight, I will be explaining the rules of our little game to her, and then it's her choice when she wants to abide by them and ultimately leave.

CHAPTER 9

ADELINE

IT'S BEEN THREE days since I first arrived...or I think so at least. I've been trying to keep track of the days and nights as best as I can. Meals are delivered periodically throughout the day by young women that so far only speak Spanish. I tried to ask for help several times, but they disregard me completely. And the one time I tried to escape, I was manhandled by a guard posted outside my door and thrown back into the room like a bag of trash.

Let's just say I learned my lesson...for now.

The way the staff isn't surprised to suddenly see a crying girl locked in a room and asking for help only confirms my earlier suspicion that I'm not the first girl that's been held here against her will.

The thought makes me sick.

It's in the afternoon, and I'm lying on the bed doing my favorite hobby that I've picked up since being kidnapped --- staring at the ceiling and crying. I feel like I haven't stopped since I've arrived, but I can't help it. I miss my home and Gio. Perhaps most of all, I miss my books. I was accustomed to being holed up in my room at home a lot, but at least I had a book to keep me company, a far-off world to escape to when I needed to the most.

Sniffling, I sit up suddenly when I hear the familiar beeping and click of the door. An older woman with short, curly salt-and-pepper hair walks into the room, her brown eyes finding me right away. She's wearing a black and white maid's uniform with no shoes. I've noted all of the maids and servants before her also have not worn any footwear, which I find to be strange.

I haven't seen this particular maid before, but she exudes a presence about her that tells me she's in charge. Staring at her in silence, I wait to see what she wants before I start asking her for help. I have no idea who I can trust here, but so far no one has offered their assistance. This woman will probably be no different.

"Hello," she says in accented English.

My eyes widen in surprise. "Y-you speak English?" I ask her, astonished.

The woman narrows her eyes at me and holds her hand up as I scramble off the bed towards her. "Before you even ask, *stupid little girl*, I am not going to do anything you request. I'm not a slave to be at your beck and call. I am only here to get you ready for dinner tonight with Master Lucien."

Master Lucien. I still haven't discovered his last name. But he probably doesn't want me to know it so I can't identify him after I escape. And I'm determined that I *will* escape.

I think back to what she said. She wants me to get ready for dinner tonight with the man that kidnapped me? I don't think so. But before I can protest, the woman is yanking on my hand and pulling me towards the bathroom. She's incredibly strong even though she's a few inches shorter than me. But what she lacks in height, she certainly makes up for in width and muscle.

"You girls are all the same," she mutters, but it's loud enough for me to hear her. "You're always so resistant to do what you're told, but then you eventually give in." She turns to me and glares at me. "Why don't you just give in and save me the trouble?"

Give in to what? I ask myself. *To being kidnapped and held against my will?*

I'm about to snap at her; but then I see the weariness in her gaze, and I suddenly feel sorry for the woman. She reminds me of the nanny I had when I was a little girl. She always looked so worse for wear, but always kept a smile on her face even though I could see her true feelings in her eyes. I truly believe a person's eyes are the windows to their souls. And I believe that even more so since I gazed into the soul of the devil who's keeping me here.

Furrowing my brows, I snatch my hand away from her when she starts pulling me again. I step past her towards the bathroom. "I'll take a shower," I tell her over my shoulder. "Will you...will you pick out something for me to wear?" I ask. I almost add because I don't know what Lucien would like me to wear, but I don't because I don't give a shit what he likes or doesn't. But it may be easier for me if she just picks out the attire. I don't know if this Lucien has a temper or not, and I certainly don't want to find out by doing something wrong.

When the woman doesn't answer, I look back at her. She's standing there with her mouth gaped, opening and closing like a fish out of water. When she notices me staring, she snaps her mouth shut. "Why isn't it always this easy?" she asks herself as she disappears into the closet.

As I step into the hot shower, the woman's words return to me; and I'm completely unsettled by them. She confirmed that there have been girls before me, but how many? And more importantly, what happened to them?

CHAPTER 10

LUCIEN

NUMBER SEVEN TOOK a long shower once again. This time it was only forty-three minutes, but that's only because the head of my staff, Maria, pounded on the door and insisted that the girl get dressed for dinner.

I chuckle to myself as I think back to the interaction between the two of them. Maria can be intimidating, to say the least. She has been like a mother figure to me for many years, even though I couldn't possibly love her like one.

I could never love anyone, for that matter. *Ever.*

Maria has been with me the longest, so she's in charge of the entire household from what meals are prepared and who cooks them down to who cleans the toilets. She definitely runs the show, and it makes my mind rest a little easier knowing she would never let the staff slack. If it's not done with perfection, she's unsatisfied, knowing that I would most definitely be unsatisfied.

I have been diagnosed with a lot of things, the most prominent being obsessive compulsive disorder. I also have a preoccupation with germs, since it kind of goes hand in hand, making for an interesting combination. Needless to say, I require everything pure, untouched and in order. And I need complete and utter control of everything and everyone around me. If I don't have those things…well, it can get very ugly.

I'm pulled from my thoughts at the sound of approaching footsteps. Maria enters the large dining hall first, followed by a clearly reluctant Number Seven. Maria tells me in Spanish that she's going to fetch the first course, and I give her a nod to dismiss her.

Seven looks nervous, twisting her fingers around her left ring finger. She must be doing this absentmindedly; because when she looks down, a frown appears on her face, and she immediately stops. When she lifts her chin and her gaze meets mine, she takes my breath away.

Maria picked out an emerald green dress, which suits the girl's hourglass figure perfectly and brings out the green of her eyes. Her long, thick, dark locks cascade down her shoulders and back, and I can't seem to tear my gaze away from her beautiful, flawless face. Her olive skin looks soft like silk, and my fingertips twitch against my thighs as the thought of finding out exactly what it feels like under my touch.

I don't ever remember being this attracted to a woman before, and I find myself anxious to even be near her. *Another first.*

Standing, I pull out the chair adjacent to mine at the head of the table and wait for her to come to me. This is a test. And she will be tested often while she's here.

Some of the previous girls thought they would come here and be the boss of me or the boss of my staff, but that is not how this works. I want them compliant and respectful…and *impeccable.* I demand their perfection.

It's what I paid for, after all.

She hesitates at first, but then she eventually begins to cross the room towards me. The dress hugs every curve of her luscious body, her hips swaying slightly as she walks. She's walking timidly and on her tiptoes as if she's used to wearing high heels.

I don't allow shoes to be worn in my home, and Maria always instructs the girls of that fact.

She stops about a foot from the chair and stares at me. Our gazes lock in a tense-filled moment before I gesture for her to sit in the chair I presented to her. She hesitates a moment longer before finally pressing her delectable ass into the plush chair. I gently push her in until she's at a comfortable distance from the table before I take my own seat just several inches to her left.

The table is long and seats fifteen. She could have sat anywhere really, but I want her close to me. I want to enjoy her since our time here is, unfortunately, limited.

"Hello. You look lovely," I tell her, hoping for a response, but disappointedly not receiving one.

I want to hear the sound of her voice. I talked to her on the first night, but she was just waking up out of a drug-induced fog and no doubt in pain. I imagine her voice to be melodic, and I can't wait until she decides to finally speak to me.

The girl simply tears her gaze away and stares at the empty plate before her.

Frowning, I grab a freshly laundered linen napkin and place it on my lap. Then I unbutton my cufflinks and methodically roll up the sleeves of my dress shirt over my strong forearms, being careful to roll each side the same number of times. I lost my suit jacket a while ago, having been too anxious and overheated while waiting for her arrival to dinner.

The first course, a cream soup, is served a few short moments later.

Seven stares at her bowl as if something is going to jump out and grab her. Hesitantly, she picks up her spoon, and I watch her hand tremble as she dips the utensil into the soup and slowly brings it to her mouth.

"Am I making you nervous?" My deep voice echoes in the large room, causing the girl to jump and dribble soup down the side of her mouth and chin.

Normally, the sight of food on someone's face would have me retching uncontrollably, but the fear in her eyes at doing something wrong has me concentrating on nothing but her reaction to me. Clearing my throat and surprising even myself, I grab one of the extra linen napkins from the table and gently wipe the soup from her pretty face.

"I didn't mean to frighten you," I whisper as I make sure every drop is wiped up. Her eyes are wide and trained on me, her breath coming out in short gasps, caressing my hand. My eye twitches as I begin to think about where her mouth has been. How many people has she kissed? How many cocks have been in that filthy mouth; juices and fluids and…? So many questions swirl around in my mind until I can't concentrate.

And that's when it happens.

My fingers accidentally graze across her lips, and it's like an electric shock going through me. I snatch my hand back and toss the used napkin to the floor.

I'm barely able to gain control of myself as my mind races, thinking about her breath on my fingertips and the fact that I touched her mouth…her mouth that is crawling with bacteria. I squeeze my eyes shut, reciting in my mind what the tests showed me earlier. I have the damn paperwork memorized. She's clean. *She's been tested; she's clean*, I tell myself over and over.

Nevertheless, I grab a bottle of hand sanitizer from my pants pocket and apply it liberally to my hands. I know I won't be able to continue on with my meal until I do so. I rub the antiseptic-smelling liquid into every crease and crevice, making sure that I get every inch of skin that may have been in contact with her.

After a while, I'm able to settle myself down enough that my heart stops racing and my breathing returns to normal. When I look up, I realize the girl's staring at me, wide-eyed and open-mouthed. It's making me feel extremely uneasy, so I clear my throat and tell her sternly, "Eat."

Her head bows and her eyes meet the table as she grasps her spoon in her trembling hand and eventually scoops a mouthful to her lips. This time she doesn't spill a drop, and I'm pleased. In fact, she continues to eat quite eloquently, almost as if she's been trained.

We make it through the first course without talking, both of us consumed with our own thoughts. I'm angry that I almost had a meltdown in front of her. I don't let the women I purchase see that side of me. None of them had any idea that I'm…not normal. They didn't spend enough time with me to determine that.

But Seven knows now. I could see the confusion and *pity* in her gaze. I clench my left hand into a fist under the table, trying to ease my temper. I don't need anyone's fucking pity.

One of my staff comes to clear our bowls --- fine china that will be uncoremoniously tossed out in the trash. I never eat from the same plate or drink from the same glass twice. The utensils are sterling silver and hand washed before being put into a high-pressure, high-temp, industrial-sized dishwasher and ultimately polished dry, so I do allow the staff to clean and reuse them. But everything else must go in the trash as a one-time use only.

My gaze keeps straying to Seven. I can't stop staring at her, and I'm sure it's making her uncomfortable, but I don't care. *She's mine to do with whatever I please*, I tell myself. But I don't know if I truly believe that.

As her delicate hand grips the crystal stemware to bring the glass of wine to her lips, I suppress a groan. I watch as she parts her lips and presses them to the rim of the glass before drinking a long sip of the very expensive and very vintage wine. Even though I just freaked out a few moments ago when I touched those very lips, I can't help but want to know what it would feel like to press my own against hers. I've never kissed anyone before or ever wanted to, for that matter, so I can't say that I know exactly what it would feel like. Her lips are full, like two soft pillows with a perfect cupid's bow.

"What's your name?" I find myself asking her even though I never bothered to care what the other women's real names were until they were leaving. And I never called the other girls by anything but their number.

I always kept it cool and impersonal from the start when it all began with the first, Number One.

"Adeline," she says in a throaty whisper, and her gaze finally meets mine.

Adeline.

Seven. Seven letters in her name. It's almost like it's fate.

She carefully picks up a linen napkin and dabs at that luscious mouth I can't stop staring at. Her pink tongue darts out to lick and wet her lips, and I can feel my thickening cock straining against my suit pants.

Once again, I'm surprised by the level of attraction I have towards this girl. Her predecessors were pretty. Some might have even called them beautiful. But Adeline is in her own separate category --- absolute perfection.

The main course is served, momentarily distracting me from my perusal of my guest, and I'm pleased to see that Maria has gone all out for this evening's meal. She's made a delicious roast with vegetables.

I grip my fork and knife in my hand and watch as Adeline does the same. However, her gaze lingers on the sharp knife. I can't help but wonder if she would try to kill me with it. The thought of blood spilling onto the floor makes me physically ill, and I squeeze my eyes shut, trying to block out the unwanted thoughts. My heart races as I think of every possible scenario that could happen with that single knife, the blade piercing my skin and infecting me with all sorts of airborne viruses and germs.

When I can't seem to suppress my runaway thoughts, I open my eyes to find Adeline staring at me once more. Our gazes lock as my chest rises and falls rapidly with panicked breaths.

She slowly sets down her utensils as if knowing exactly what I need in that moment. With the knife and ultimate threat out of her reach, it sends an immediate wash of calmness over me. My eyes search her gorgeous face, and I can feel my heartbeat begin to slow. Focusing on her helps me, I realize. It allows me to ward off my demons temporarily, and the relief I'm feeling because of her is unexpected. My breathing slowly returns to normal, and I force myself to focus on the meal before me.

That's twice now you freaked out in front of her, I mentally chide myself.

I stare at the food before me, not sure whether I'm still feeling hungry or not. Out of the corner of my eye, I watch as Adeline picks up just her fork and spears a small carrot. She brings the vegetable up to her mouth and chews delicately.

I've never been so fascinated with someone before. It's as if every move she makes is some choreographed dance. She is flawless.

Feeling calmer by watching her eat, I slowly pick up my fork and join her in eating the delicious meal. We eat this course in silence as well; and while I'm used to the quiet, I suddenly want to hear her melodic voice again.

It takes me several tries before I'm able to ask her a question. She's reduced me to feeling like a nervous teenage boy talking to a pretty girl for the first time. "Adeline," I say, my voice sounding hoarse and needy. Her eyes snap up to meet mine, and suddenly my train of thought goes right out the window.

I can see a myriad of emotions flash through her pretty, green eyes, and then she blurts out her own question instead. "Why am I here?"

Again, her confusion frightens me. How could she possibly not know what she's gotten herself into unless… I shake my head, not wanting to think about that worrisome possibility. "I bought you."

She nods in acceptance considering I already told her on the first night that I had purchased her. "But what do you *want* from me?" she asks.

Steeling myself, because I'm fearful she truly doesn't know the answer to her question, I tell her honestly, "Your virginity."

CHAPTER 11

ADELINE

I DIDN'T KNOW what to expect when the older woman, who eventually told me her name was Maria after practically dragging it out of her, came to my room and told me to dress for dinner. *Dinner with my kidnapper.*

Facing him was going to be no easy task. Even though I'd seen him the night I was brought here, it was dark, and I was drugged. I can't clearly recall what he looks like except for the profile of a handsome face and piercing, dark eyes that make me shiver every time I think about them.

That first night when he told me he bought me, I figured he was some ruthless and demonic sadist who would tie me down and whip and torture me. The thoughts that have run through my head the past few days have made me crazy with worry. I've sat and waited for him to come for me, but he never did. And his absence only left me more confused and more nervous about what was to come.

When Maria took me to the dining room, I kept wishing for the floor to open up and swallow me whole. I'd never been so nervous in my entire life.

As I stood in the entrance to the room by myself, nervously playing with my finger, wishing I still had my engagement ring, something familiar to keep my mind at ease, I could feel his presence from across the room.

When I finally collected enough courage to face him, I almost gasped in shock. He was young, much younger than I thought he would be...and *handsome.* So incredibly handsome that he stole my breath the instant my eyes met his beautiful face.

For a brief moment, I thought that this couldn't possibly be the man who kidnapped me. It was hard to believe that a man who looked like this could be capable of such heinous proclivities.

But when I stared into his dark eyes, I remembered them immediately. Two penetrating pools of dark chocolate that seemed to intensely watch and study my every movement with a calculating gaze.

I realized that my perception of this man was completely the opposite of what I had expected, of what I'd feared.

And now, as I sit beside him at a table big enough for a large family, I can't help but steal glances at him, wondering why I'm here, why he brought me here...and when or *if* he'll let me leave.

Lucien seems dignified with manners. He's wearing a white, woven, long-sleeved dress shirt, the sleeves rolled up over his muscular forearms, with a dark green tie that matches the color of my dress.

I study him as he moves his silverware into a perfect line and places a linen napkin neatly on his lap. Everything about him screams precision. Even his dark hair, which is longer on top and shorter on the sides, is swept back off of his handsome face and gelled to perfection with not a single hair out of place.

Glancing around the large, immaculate room with antique furniture in every corner and three crystal chandeliers hanging from the high ceilings, I can't help but wonder how much Lucien actually paid for me. It's very clear that he's rich --- beyond rich. From what I have seen of this place so far, it dwarfs my father's mansion and is nothing short of majestic.

I have no idea what Lucien does for a living or why he needs to kidnap girls, and I'm hoping to find all of that out soon. But every time I try to think of a question to ask him, my throat closes up tight with anxiety. Although Lucien appears like a Greek god on the outside with his chiseled features and handsome face, he strikes me as someone who is powerful and used to getting what he wants.

And he wants me.

We start the first course, a cream soup that smells delicious. Even though my stomach is uneasy, I force myself to pick up my spoon. My hand is trembling as I dip the bowl of the spoon into the soup and slowly bring it to my mouth.

"Am I making you nervous?" His deep voice echoes off the walls in the large room, and I jump, dribbling soup down the side of my mouth and chin.

I hear his intake of breath, and I sit stock-still in my chair, so afraid of his reaction to my mishap that I can't even move. To my surprise, he grabs a linen napkin from the table and begins to wipe the liquid from my face.

Having him in such close proximity throws me into a panic. My breaths are coming out in short gasps as I stare at him, waiting for his next move. Will he hurt me now? I have no idea what his triggers are or what he intends to do with me.

"I didn't mean to frighten you," he whispers as he continues to obsessively clean my face, the napkin now chafing against my delicate skin.

His right eye twitches as my panicked breaths fill the quiet room. His lips move as he murmurs to himself, and I don't think he's even aware that he's doing it.

And then his fingers graze against my lips, and his whole demeanor instantly changes. He snatches his hand back from me as if I'd just burnt him. I watch as he leans forward in his chair, his face contorting with pain. He squeezes his eyes shut as his lips move a million miles a minute.

I stare at him in disbelief and glance around the room, wondering what the hell is happening.

How could this strong, powerful man be reduced to a mumbling, anxiety-stricken mess in the matter of a single touch?

After a few minutes, he grabs a small bottle of hand sanitizer from his pocket and squeezes a copious amount onto his hands, scrubbing and scrubbing until he covers every inch of skin on his hands and wrists.

And then, almost as quickly as the panic attack started, it's all over with. Lucien is able to eventually come back to reality and a somewhat relatively normal and calm state.

When he notices me staring at him with what is probably a shocked and confused look on my face, he tells me in a stern, unforgiving tone to eat.

I stare down at the soup in front of me and will myself to concentrate on it and not the fact that my captor is clearly unstable. His volatility scares me more than anything. He could fly off the handle over the smallest and simplest thing, and it reminds me instantly of my father. I've been walking on eggshells my entire life. And it looks like it won't be any different here.

I manage to get through the first course, thankfully, without spilling another drop.

As a young man emerges from the kitchen to clear our bowls, I wrap my fingers around the stem of the wineglass in front of me. I'm suddenly feeling very parched, and the cold, fruity wine feels good running down my dry throat.

Out of the corner of my eye, I can see that Lucien is staring at me, but I refuse to meet his gaze. He shifts in his chair, watching my every move as I set the glass down and continue to stare at the table, ignoring him until he asks me a simple question.

"What is your name?"

I almost feel relieved by his request. When one of my sisters was kidnapped and held for ransom by an enemy of my father, I befriended a retired FBI agent my father had hired to help get my sister back.

He had told me that if the same thing ever happened to me that I should try to get my captors to see me as a human being instead of an object in exchange for money. "Talk to them," he had said. "Make them see you as a person. That will make them less likely to harm you."

So in light of the knowledge I garnered from the retired agent, I decide to indulge my captor. "Adeline," I answer him in an almost whisper.

His reaction is slight, but I can see a change in him. His lips move rapidly, but I can't hear what he's saying. I think I catch the word "seven", but I'm not totally sure. It's almost as if he's thinking out loud to himself, and I can't help but wonder if he does that often.

I have a million questions I want to ask; but after the way he reacted to me earlier, I'm afraid to set him off again.

He's clearly mentally unstable. Not that I didn't think that before. I mean, he did kidnap me and is holding me prisoner, after all. I didn't exactly think he was sane…but knowing that a raging lunatic could be lurking under that handsome exterior is worrisome. Someone like that could snap at any given moment, and I have no idea what type of crazy I'm dealing with here exactly.

The staff brings out the main course, a beef roast with veggies. I watch Lucien pick up his utensils, and then I mirror his actions. I notice that the knife in my right hand is sharp, and I can't seem to tear my gaze away from the blade. It's suddenly so much more than a steak knife. This could be my way out of here.

I'm ripped from my thoughts by the sound of Lucien's panicked breaths. When I turn to him, his eyes are squeezed shut, and I realize he's having another episode. I shift uncomfortably in my seat. He looks like he's in pain, and I suddenly feel sorry for him…even though I know I most definitely shouldn't.

When his eyes open and our gazes lock, I can see the suffering in his gaze. He's undoubtedly troubled. *Very troubled.*

Not breaking our connection, I slowly set my utensils down. I know his panic started when I picked up the knife, so maybe that is what caused it. I watch him as his chest rises and falls rapidly until he eventually is able to gain control of himself.

Hesitantly, I pick up just my fork and begin to eat, noticing that his gaze is still trained on me. After a while, he finally picks up his own fork, and we eat the delicious meal in uncomfortable silence.

My mind feels like it's racing a million miles a minute, and it's driving me crazy not to blurt out a question or two.

"Adeline," Lucien says, disrupting the deafening silence.

My eyes snap up to his, and I watch as he opens his mouth just to close it again. Suddenly, unable to suffer through this any longer, I blurt out, "Why am I here?"

With a look of concern on his face, Lucien slowly shakes his head. "I bought you."

I nod in understanding; because as implausible as that disturbing piece of information may seem, he already told me that the first night I was brought here. "But what do you *want* from me?" I press even though I'm fearful of his response.

He takes a moment before answering. And when he finally does, his response floors me. "Your virginity."

My entire world seems to tilt on its axis, and all I can hear is a rush of blood in my ears as my heart threatens to beat out of my chest.

Tears immediately fill my eyes, but I blink them back, not allowing any to fall. My worst fear is coming to fruition. He kidnapped and brought me here so that he could rape me.

And the thing that hits me the hardest is that my first time won't be with my future husband. It's going to be with my captor, the man who kidnapped me, who's going to steal my innocence…and probably kill me.

I twist the linen napkin in my hands, having suddenly lost my appetite. A bitter taste forms in the back of my throat, and I'm afraid that the delicious dinner might be making another appearance.

I swallow hard to keep it down and then squeak out the question, "How much?" When he doesn't answer, I finally meet his eyes. He's staring at me, those two dark pools studying my every move and making me feel uneasy. "You said you bought me. How much did you pay?" I don't know why, but I need to know.

He doesn't even blink as he replies with, "One million dollars."

One million dollars?! My mind swims in confusion. He paid a million dollars to have me kidnapped. This feels like some kind of dream. *No.* This feels like a freaking *nightmare*.

Gritting my teeth to hold back the tears threatening to overflow, I reach for the knife and grasp it in my right hand. I remember what happened last time I had the knife in my hand. Lucien looked almost…frightened. And I realize that I want him to feel that way again. In fact, I want him to feel just one-tenth of the fear I have right in this moment.

Tears, which I tried so hard to keep from falling, now stream down my face as I slowly stand up from the table. I can feel Lucien still beside me, and then he slowly sets his fork down and places his hands on the edge of the table in a vice-like grip, turning his knuckles white.

"Adeline," he warns, and I can hear the unease in his tone.

Earlier I was thinking that there was no escape from here, but I haven't actually *tried*. Maybe I'm giving in too quickly, too soon. I at least have to *try*...especially now that I know what he's planning to do to me.

Lucien suddenly stands, knocking his chair over in the process. It clangs to the floor, the noise echoing against the walls.

I grip the handle tight in my palm and point the blade towards him. "Don't come near me," I hiss at him.

Lucien swallows hard, his Adam's apple bobbing in his thick throat. He's nervous. For some reason, knives make him nervous.

Good, I think to myself. I'm going to use this to my advantage in every way possible.

Regardless of the fear he might be feeling at this moment, he still steps towards me. I jerk the knife towards him, the blade swishing in the air and only missing him by a centimeter. His eyes meet mine, and the look on his face is murderous.

Not wanting to waste another minute in this godforsaken place, I run towards the door where I've seen the servers coming in and out of all evening. I push through the swinging door and wind up in a huge kitchen, which is bigger than most people's apartments.

The staff is all hard at work, not even noticing that I entered. My feet move swiftly as I move past the cooks and servers. Towards the back of the room, I notice Maria at the same time she spots me.

She calls out something in Spanish, and I can hear the surprise in her voice.

As a result of her shouting, a tall, dark-haired man, who is sitting at the side of the room eating at a table, looks up. Our eyes lock in an unwavering gaze. He looks American with piercing, gray eyes. He's not as tall as

Lucien, but similar in looks --- dark hair and devastatingly handsome.

The man's brows furrow when he sees the knife in my hand, and he stands. "What are you doing in here?" he asks me.

His steel-gray eyes catch me off-guard with a sense of familiarity. A memory of my capture comes rushing back to me.

Gentle hands, gray eyes...a deep voice whispering, "Just a little pinch. This will only hurt for a second."

This is the man who drugged me and brought me here. I'm sure of it.

He takes a few steps towards me with an apprehensive expression on his face. Quickly, I hold my knife out, warding him off.

"Easy," he says, putting his hands up defensively and taking a step back.

"I want to leave," I plead with him. "Just let me go."

He seems amused by my request. "Sure. The door's right over there," he says, hooking his thumb behind him to the far wall where I see a door that could possibly lead to the outside world.

I stare at him for a beat, wondering if this is some kind of trick, but the smirk on his face doesn't waver.

Not wanting to waste another moment and risk being captured again, I hightail it to the door, turning the handle and throwing my weight against the heavy steel. The door opens with no problem, and I can hear the man call after me, "Hope you're not too disappointed."

I don't even have time to register what he means; because the moment fresh air hits my face, I just want to cry at the sensation. It feels like forever rather than just a few days since I've been outside.

I take off running, trying to put as much distance between me and them as possible. Not even glancing back, I tear off in the grassy lawn, running through field after field of vegetables and fruit trees, my legs pumping as hard as they will go. It's dark, but there are motion-detector lights throughout the property that come on periodically, lighting my way.

I come to several large greenhouses and keep moving. It looks like the thick grass ends several yards ahead, but I can't see what's beyond that. With the moon hidden behind stormy clouds, it just looks like a black pool of darkness.

My bare feet skid to a halt right at the end of the grass, but I end up falling forward and down over the edge. I roll on what feels like sand and rocks, scraping my arms and legs in the process until I finally come to a stop and losing the knife.

When I gain my composure, I manage to stand. And that's when my heart sinks.

Water. I'm surrounded by…water.

I run towards the waves lapping at the sandy beach, and stare out over the dark liquid. All I see is a sea of obscurity. No lights, no houses, no land. *Nothing.* I turn, staring down one side of the beach and then the other.

There's nothing. No escape.

"No," I whisper, my voice wavering. Balling my hands into fists, I scream against the wind whipping against my face, "No!"

And then that's when I hear *his* voice behind me. "The only way on and off of this island is by a small plane. I take it you don't know how to fly, do you, Adeline?" he asks with a snarl.

I spin around to glare at Lucien. "Where am I? " I demand.

"On a private island far off the Mediterranean coast." A smug smirk appears on his face.

In that very moment, I wish I still had the knife within my grasp. I don't know if I honestly could ever hurt someone…or even kill someone, but I want to hurt Lucien. I want him to know how much he's hurting me.

Just then, two dark figures appear behind my captor. He snaps his fingers, and they move towards me. "No! Don't touch me!" I scream as they grab me, holding me tightly in their grasps. As they carry me past Lucien, I scream at him, "I hate you! I hate you!", the words tearing from my throat.

He stares out at the water, seemingly unfazed by my screams, and it only infuriates me more.

I don't stop fighting and screaming until the two guards unceremoniously throw me into the bedroom I've been locked in for days.

They slam the door shut, and the keypad beeps, signaling that I'm locked in here once again.

I pound my fists against the door, yanking on the door knob and screaming until my voice is hoarse.

But no one comes for me.

No one will ever come for me, I tell myself.

Tears fill my eyes, and I can't stop them from falling down my cheeks. My escape from the mansion was easy…far too easy. I should have figured that they wouldn't just let me go.

That man, the one who helped kidnap me, knew I wouldn't be able to go anywhere. I'm a strong swimmer, but I would never be able to make it to the mainland alive. Who knows how many miles I would have to swim in order to achieve that goal…and that's if I don't get eaten in the process.

No. The only way off of this island is either by boat or plane, and I don't have the means to get to either one of those, let alone know how to operate them.

I'm stuck here.

Feeling defeated, I walk over to the bed and collapse, sinking into the soft mattress and crying myself to sleep.

CHAPTER 12

LUCIEN

"I HATE YOU! I hate you!"

I cringe as Adeline's words on the beach repeat over and over again in my head like a torturous, broken record.

It's not like I haven't heard those words before. My mother used to tell me that at least once a day when I was a child. I thought I was numb to that kind of thing, but Adeline makes me...*feel*. There's something about her that brings out this myriad of emotions and feelings that I can't make heads or tails of.

She hates me. She has every reason to hate me...but I realize I don't want her to. And when she screamed those words, it was as if she really had taken that knife and gutted me right there on the ground.

Chasing her onto the beach...my bare feet in the sand and rocks...I still can't believe I did that. I rarely step foot outside of this house, let alone go to the beach barefooted where anything can wash ashore and little creatures could crawl on me at any moment.

Running after her didn't even make me hesitate, because she was the only thing I could think about and focus on. She made me forget everything else, all of my obsessive fears and intrusive thoughts.

And that is something that has never happened before.

After I made sure Adeline was safe and secured in her room, I took a long shower, scrubbing my body under scalding water for hours until my skin was raw and bleeding. Even after I was done, I still didn't feel clean.

Now, I sit at my monitor, staring at her on the camera feed. She's finally calmed down after a fit of rage when my men first threw her in there.

A nagging feeling in the back of my mind is telling me this is more than just her second-guessing her decision to come here. It's as if she has no recollection at all…or maybe she never knew.

And if she doesn't know…then that means I'm possibly keeping an innocent girl here against her will and that she will never give me what I paid for.

There's a soft knock at my office door before Jackson inputs the code to my office. A scowl is on my face when he walks in.

I don't need a fucking lecture right now.

"What in the hell happened tonight?" he hisses the question after closing the door.

"I don't know," I tell him honestly.

"You've had girls who have changed their minds before, but they've never gone to the extremes of wanting to leave…or gut the staff…including you."

I rest my elbows on my desk, put my head in my hands and sigh. "I have no fucking idea what's wrong with her. At first I thought maybe she hit her head too hard ---."

"She did have one nasty blow to the temple. And the bruises…" His voice trails off. "You don't think she…"

Jax doesn't finish his thought. I know what he's thinking. It's the exact same thing that I've been thinking.

"I paid her handler," I tell my cousin through gritted teeth. "Everything is the same as before. If she wants to back out now ---." I shake my head. "I need more time. I need more information," I tell him, turning to him.

He has an uneasy look on his face, but he nods in understanding. "If she came here against her will, Luc, then you'd be breaking all the rules you set up in the first place."

I nod solemnly.

"Get some rest," he tells me, but we both know I won't sleep a wink tonight.

I watch him leave before sighing loudly and staring up at the ceiling. Tomorrow, I will talk to Adeline and find out the truth. I want to know what she knows and what she doesn't. And then I will need to come to a decision…although it feels like a decision has already been made.

The dark monster inside of me has already dug its claws into Adeline and claimed her as his.

And I don't know if I will ever be able to let her go until I get what I want.

CHAPTER 13

ADELINE

THE NEXT DAY I take a long bath, finding solace in the warm water. My throat still hurts from screaming myself hoarse last night, and my eyes feel swollen and sore from crying so much.

I lean my head against the tiled wall and sigh deeply. I feel physically and emotionally exhausted, and I've been here less than a week. How much longer can I keep this up?

The conversation we had over dinner last night replays in my mind. A nagging feeling in the back of my mind keeps telling me to just give in to him so I can leave. But how could I live with myself afterwards? I can't even imagine having sex with a total stranger, let alone my *kidnapper*.

I think back to last night and the way I screamed at Lucien that I hated him. I still can't believe I said that to the man who holds my fate in his hands.

He could kill me and not even think twice about it.

Lucien is obviously a very powerful and influential man. He has a mansion on a private island in the middle of nowhere apparently, and his hundred or so staff is completely loyal to the man…or should I say *monster*.

Feeling defeated, I step out of the tub and drain the water. I quickly dry off and wrap one towel around my hair and a second one around my body before walking into the bedroom to find something to wear. My steps falter as I realize I'm not alone.

Sitting in one of the occasional chairs in the corner of the room is Lucien. He's wearing a black button up shirt and black trousers, and his hair is slicked back and gelled neatly again.

I can't help but stare at his bare feet and wonder why he forbids shoes to be worn by anyone in his home. Maria had instructed me not to wear footwear last night for dinner even though there were a few pairs of high heels in the closet. She hadn't offered an explanation as to the reasoning behind that request.

When I look up, I realize he's shamelessly perusing my towel-covered body. I cinch the towel tighter around me and glare at him when he meets my eyes finally.

Did he come here to rape me? Is he going to take what he bought?

I swallow hard past the lump forming in my throat, and I take a few steps back towards the bathroom.

Lucien stands and puts his hands up defensively. "I won't touch you. I just came to talk," he says in a soft voice, as if he's afraid he'll frighten me away.

I watch as he tucks his hands into his pockets and stands still, his dark eyes piercing mine. They are like two black, unwavering pits, giving me a glimpse of the dark, disturbed soul lying underneath.

A tear cascades down my cheek, and he watches it, transfixed on its movement. "Are you…are you going to…" I choke on my words, holding back a sob. I can't even manage to get the nasty, unthinkable word out of my mouth. It's lodged deep in my throat. And in a way, I feel like if I don't say it out loud, maybe it won't happen.

"I don't rape women," he says coldly, clearly getting my meaning. "I didn't get a chance to explain the rules to you before you...before you ruined dinner."

Before I ruined dinner? I think to myself. I'd like to know what he thinks any other woman in my situation would have done. Surely the women he kept here before me didn't give him what he wanted without a fight.

"I'm not sure what your handler told you was going to happen, but this is not the way things work around here. You don't get to back out of our deal because you're having second thoughts."

I'm stunned into silence as I try to make sense of what he's telling me. I kind of feel like I'm in a room full of people and am the only one not getting the joke.

He hesitates for a moment before telling me, "The sooner you come to me and give me what I bought and want, the sooner you get paid and go home."

I stare at him in disbelief. "Y-you would l-let me go?" I stammer, my entire body trembling.

He nods once. "I let the other women before you go home as well."

His words hit me hard. I already knew there had been others. He has had sex with multiple other girls that he's kept prisoner...probably in the same room I've been sleeping in. "How many?" I ask, suddenly needing to know the answer.

"Six."

That makes me number seven.

"And you let all of them go right after you...after you were done?" I ask, not even being able to say the word.

"Every. Single. One," he says, enunciating each word to me.

I narrow my eyes at him, feeling skeptical. "How do I know you're telling me the truth?"

After a brief pause, he tells me, "Why would I lie? I have no reason to."

So he kidnaps women, brings them here to his island. And then, as soon as he sleeps with them, he lets them go. It makes no sense. Why go through all that trouble, unless... "Were all the women virgins?" I ask.

"Of course," he says as if I should know this already.

Some of the pieces of this giant puzzle are starting to click in place, but Lucien really is an enigma wrapped inside a riddle. I can't make heads or tails of him or his erratic behavior. I feel like I'm really missing the bigger picture here.

The promise of going home appeals to me, but I would have to sleep with him to gain my freedom. The thought of having sex with a stranger, especially the man who is responsible for kidnapping me and holding me against my will, makes me physically ill.

I feel bile rising up the back of my throat, and I have to swallow hard to keep it down. If he stays true to his word, then having sex with him once will get me what I want most in the world right now --- my freedom.

Could I actually go through with this? Could I actually betray my soon-to-be husband? What would Gio think of me if he learned that I didn't save myself for our wedding night? He probably wouldn't even want me anymore.

And my father...oh, god, my father would probably kill me...if I don't wind up dead on this island long before that.

I release a shaky sigh from between my parted lips as I meet the eyes of my kidnapper. "What happens if I don't want to sleep with you?" I ask, my question just above a whisper.

"Then you don't go home," he says, his tone cold and detached.

"You would keep me here? Forever?" I ask, disbelieving. Surely, if Lucien doesn't get what he wants, he would eventually let me go. But as soon as the thought rolls around in my mind, I already know my answer before he even speaks.

"If that's what it took...yes," he answers calmly. "I'm very good at waiting for what I want," he adds. Then he pulls his hands out of his pockets and checks the expensive-looking watch on his wrist, appearing to be bored with me and this little chat of ours, and it makes me furious.

His eyes meet mine as he says, "The sooner you give me what I paid for, the sooner you can leave. It's that simple."

And then he turns and leaves, locking me inside this room once again and leaving me spinning with the knowledge that he holds the only key to my freedom.

* * * * * * *

THAT EVENING OVER dinner, Lucien's words echo over and over again in my brain, bouncing against my skull and reverberating until it's the only thing I can hear and focus on.

The sooner you give me what I want, the sooner you can leave.

But how could I possibly give my virginity to this man? I would remember it for the rest of my life, and that thought alone sends fear straight through me like an icy dagger in my spine. I can't do this.

Spending all day in solitude with only my thoughts and worst fears keeping me company is starting to make me feel crazy.

I miss Giovanni.

I miss my room and my things.

I even miss my father. Well, maybe only a tiny bit.

I want to go home. But could I really commit this sickening act with someone I don't even know and deep down loathe? Emily, a girl I knew back in high school, told me that you always remember your first. I most definitely would remember this regardless of it being my first time or not. The circumstances are heinous, and I wouldn't want to remember any of it, but I would be forced to. This is something my mind would play over and over again until I either got psychological help or shoved it so far down into my subconscious that it never resurfaced again.

Can I actually go through with this?

At this point…I don't think I have a choice. He's not going to let me go until I give him what he wants, what he *paid* for. So, maybe I should just get it over with. I can deal with the consequences and mental anguish later.

"Adeline?"

His deep timbre brings me back to the present. When I meet his gaze, his dark brows furrow. "Are you not hungry?" he asks.

I glance down at the chicken dish in front of me. I had been daydreaming for so long that I haven't even taken one bite of it yet.

Instead of having dinner downstairs in the dining room, my meals have all been in my room the past few days. When Maria and another member of the staff brought in a table and two chairs around dinnertime, I asked her what was going on.

"You're having dinner with Master Lucien in your room tonight," she had told me.

I didn't even have to ask her why. I knew why. No one trusted me to not try to run away again…even though I couldn't possibly get away. I know that now.

And as I glance down at my plastic utensils sans knife, of course, I know that Lucien doesn't trust me either. But if I have any hope of getting off of this island, I need to gain his trust.

Using my fork, I spear the piece of chicken and tear off a piece before sticking it in my mouth and chewing slowly. The meat is so tender that I don't even need anything stronger than a plastic fork, thankfully.

I can feel Lucien's stare on me as I eat. He's always staring. Always watching. And it's unnerving.

With as much resolve as I manage to muster, I meet his stare. "Were you serious about letting the other girls go after you…after you were finished with them?" I ask, almost choking on the words.

His eyes narrow for a moment before he answers. "Yes. Of course."

Slowly, I set my fork down and swallow hard, fighting down the urge to vomit. Hanging my head in shame, I whisper, "I'm…I'm ready now."

I feel a heated blush creeping up my chest and to my face as I feel Lucien's intense stare on me. I expect him to stand up and attack me like a wild animal, but he remains seated and quiet.

When I finally get the courage to look at him, he has an unreadable expression on his face. He grips the delicate stem of the wine glass in his powerful hand and takes a long swig of the red liquid.

Every movement he makes is like a choreographed dance --- practiced, thoroughly planned out and perfectly executed. He exudes confidence and power, but there is something about his eyes that make me think he wasn't always this way. I can see the same emotion behind those dark orbs that I see reflected in my own quite often --- pain and fear.

When he finally sets down his glass, he utters the exact opposite of what I had been expecting him to say.

"You're not ready yet."

"W-what?" I falter. Here I was ready to give myself to him, and now he's telling me no? I don't get it. He doesn't think I'm ready yet? I'll *never* be ready. Surely he has to understand that.

Feeling embarrassed by throwing myself at him, I shrink into myself, not able to meet his eyes. The promise of going home is flying out of my reach with every passing moment, and I just want this all to end. "Don't you...don't you want me?" I ask, finally getting the courage to meet his stare.

His dark, broody eyes devour me. "Of course I do," he says confidently. "But you're not ready to give me what I want, Adeline."

The sound of my name coming from his mouth causes me to shudder. Quickly, I admonish my traitorous body for feeling any sort of attraction towards my kidnapper. It's just *wrong*. So very wrong.

After a few more moments of silence, Lucien finally speaks. "Eat," he demands before turning his attention back to his food.

I watch him for several seconds before stabbing a piece of chicken with my plastic fork. I chew the meat angrily, fuming over what just took place.

CHAPTER 14

LUCIEN

ADELINE SEEMS TO finally understand the rules now. She doesn't appear to be *playing dumb* anymore, which is a relief.

And the sooner I get what I want, the sooner I can get her out of my fucking system and the sooner I can send her away.

She has turned my world nearly upside down in the short time she's been here, and I can't imagine making this a long-term thing.

"You would keep me here? Forever?"

Her question makes me grin. I lied when I said I would keep her here forever, and she was naïve enough to believe me. I like to think that eventually I would grow tired of her games and return her to New York, but a small part of me wonders if that's true.

I never waited long with the other women, but none of them truly toyed with me or tested me the way Adeline has. Most were in a rush to get our transaction over with. Only one thought she could stay here with me, but she knew the rules. I don't keep used goods.

Adeline is stalling and proving to be difficult, and I don't know why. I'm not even sure if I really want to know the reasons behind her hesitation.

I went into her room this morning with the intention of finding out as much as I could about why she's really here and the reason behind her confusion, but then I found myself ignoring the elephant in the room.

She seemed a little confused and asked some peculiar questions as if she didn't understand what is expected of her here, but I blame that on her handler. Morello clearly didn't explain everything to Adeline that he was supposed to. But considering he emailed me right before the deadline, he was most likely in a rush.

Criminals only care about money, not about the people they hurt in the process. I know that better than anyone.

Honestly, I don't want to know why she doesn't want to be here and don't care if she has ultimately changed her mind, because I fucking want her.

I want her more than my next breath.

This girl has crawled under my skin and rooted herself deep inside my veins, and I know I can't just let her go without first taking what I want.

My dark obsession with her frightens me. I've never felt like this before, and I've never craved anything the way I crave Adeline.

It took every single ounce of my willpower to stay in my seat when she offered herself to me during dinner. I wanted to rip her clothes off and plunge my rock hard cock into her silky depths. I had an insanely feral reaction to that girl. And if she could have heard all the depraved thoughts that raced through my mind when she told me she was ready, she would have run screaming the other way.

But one look into her eyes after her offer told me everything I needed to know. She was scared. And she certainly didn't want me.

That instantly calmed the dark beast inside of me from taking her; because for some sick reason, I want Adeline to offer herself to me. I want her to be attracted to me.

I want her to want me just one-tenth of how much I fucking want her.

And the idea of such a painstakingly beautiful creature wanting me turns me the fuck on.

I'm not going to give her a chance to change her mind and back out of our deal. I've already decided I'm going to have her and take what I want.

Consequences be damned.

I just hope she doesn't make me wait much longer.

CHAPTER 15

ADELINE

LUCIEN AND I continue to play the cat and mouse game over the next several days. I try to lure him into my web of lies and deceit so that I can go home, but he always resists.

The more he turns me down, the more I try. And I'm starting to think that maybe this was his goal all along.

We have dinner in my room again just like we have for the past few evenings, and I decide to try a different approach. Instead of asking when I can go home and basically eating in silence, I'm going to make some small-talk and get to know my captor a little better...even if that should be the furthest thing from my mind right now.

If I'm being totally honest with myself, Lucien's company hasn't been...awful. He's actually seems really smart, and he is nice to look at. I don't know why I'm trying to find the silver lining in this messed up situation, but at least he's not an old, ugly, bald guy with a pot belly who's trying to rape me every night.

Things could definitely be worse.

I need to keep telling myself that if I'm going to survive this.

"What do you do for a living, Lucien?" I ask him while stabbing a buttered asparagus spear with my plastic fork. Apparently, I'm still not being trusted with metal utensils.

Lucien dabs his mouth with a linen napkin. "Without getting into too many boring details, I'm a software engineer."

"So you're good with computers then."

"Yes."

"Did you go to college for that?" I'm genuinely interested, and I hope that he can see that.

"Yes and no. I went to college, but dropped out to pursue other ventures. I was trained by a professional hacker to perform some of the work I need to do."

I absorb the information slowly. That explains how he was able to kidnap me from so far away. With his money, power and skills, I'm sure his reach is unlimited.

"I see," I say softly, turning my attention back to my meal. Everything is cooked perfectly and tastes delicious, as usual. Grasping the stem of my wine glass, I bring it to my mouth and sip the cool, red liquid.

Over the rim of the glass, I can see Lucien watching my every move. His eyes are hooded and focused on my mouth. He does this often while we eat, and it's as if he enjoys watching me do mundane things like talking, eating and drinking.

It's obvious that he's attracted to me. I would imagine that if he wasn't, he would have never decided to kidnap me. So why is he making it so difficult for me to take him up on his offer so that I can go home?

I set the glass back down, and his dark chocolate eyes track my movement. He looks devastatingly handsome tonight in a tailored three-piece dark suit and tie. His hair is perfectly styled, like always, and his strong jaw is clean-shaven. I've never seen him having so much as a five-o'clock shadow.

He exudes perfection, but I wonder if his appearance is by choice or if it was ingrained upon him, like in my case. What I would have given to be able to wear sweatpants around the house and throw my hair up into a messy bun. I was never allowed to look less than flawless at all times, no matter what. My father's rules were harsh, to say the least. And I can't say that I miss them at all.

If anything, I wish I never had to return to the prison my father calls our home.

Lucien had mentioned about paying me before he released me, and that's been nagging at the back of my mind. I wonder how much money he's talking about. Maybe I wouldn't have to return back to my prison at all. Maybe I could start a new life with the money.

"Lucien," I start, and I watch as his eyes darken. "You...you mentioned paying me before letting me go." After he nods in agreement, I shyly ask, "How much?"

He leans back in his chair and considers my question for a moment. "I'm presuming your handler didn't give you any money?"

I tilt my head to the side as I try to understand what he means by handler once again. Maybe he means the guys who kidnapped me at gunpoint. I simply shake my head, not giving him a verbal answer since I definitely didn't receive anything other than sheer terror that night.

He frowns in clear disappointment. "I figured as much." He takes a moment before saying, "One million."

My eyes widen at his words. He's going to give me...one million dollars to sleep with him? "Why?" The question blurts out of my mouth before I can even stop myself.

"Why what?"

"Why would you pay me that much money? Why are you the way you are?" I ask, the questions tumbling out one after another.

He shakes his head, and I know I won't get an answer out of him. "I just am," he whispers, but I can hear the sadness in his voice.

"You could have any woman you want," I say, my mouth clearly not waiting for my brain to tell it to shut up.

My compliment seems to amuse him, though, and I see a ghost of a smile on his mouth before it disappears altogether. I don't think I've ever seen him genuinely smile. And I most certainly have never heard him laugh. He's always so serious...so detached from everyone around him and the outside world.

My mind races for a reason. There has to be a reason for why he's like this. If I can find out, maybe it will make me...hate him less.

"You'll never figure it out," he tells me as if reading my thoughts. "No one ever has, and I don't expect you to now. My past isn't any concern of yours, and I'd like to keep it right where it is...in the past," he says sternly. "It doesn't matter now," he says softly, and I can hear the hurt in his tone.

But I think he's lying. I think it does matter. Somehow his past shaped him into the man he is today. All of his eccentricities add up to something bigger. Something traumatic happened to him...or maybe someone hurt him.

Suddenly, I think he and I have a lot more in common than I ever thought. And the urge to comfort him hits me out of the blue.

Throwing all rational thought out the window, I reach across the table and place my hand over his.

And then all hell breaks loose.

Snatching his hand back as if he's just been burnt by my touch, Lucien suddenly stands, knocking his chair over in the process and rattling the table enough that several things spill, including the wine, onto the white, pristine tablecloth. A sheer look of terror is on his face as he takes in the mess, the blood red wine still slowly soaking into the cloth.

"I'm sorry. I didn't know. I didn't ---."

Lucien's eyes snap to mine, and the intense anger I see in his gaze causes me to clamp my mouth shut.

Without another word, he turns and goes to the door. It takes him three tries before he manages to type the right code into the keypad, and he profusely curses through gritted teeth after each failed attempt.

His entire body shudders in barely controlled anger as he leaves, slamming the door shut behind him.

I'm standing in the middle of the room with my mouth agape for a very long time after he disappears trying to figure out what the hell I did wrong.

CHAPTER 16

LUCIEN

I LEAVE ADELINE'S room and go straight to my shower --- my sanctuary.

Panicked breaths spill out from my lungs as I crank on the hot water and strip out of my clothes. I throw them in a pile on the floor, which causes me even more anxiety, but I'm in a fucking hurry to get under the soothing spray of water.

I step into the glass enclosure and close the door, sighing in relief when the burning hot water envelops me from the large showerhead above. With frantic hands, I grab one of the antibacterial bars of soap from the built-in shelf and scrub at my hand, the place where Adeline had touched me.

Growling in anger, I scrub until my hand is red and raw. I'm not angry at Adeline, however. She has no idea of how deep-rooted my phobias are. I'm angry at myself for being this way and not being fucking normal.

I felt like we were finally making progress tonight, and then I went and fucked it all up.

A feral scream tears from my throat as the scalding water cascades down my body, turning my skin into a bright, cherry red. Mumbling to myself and counting the tiles on the wall beside me, I scrub and scrub until I can no longer stand it, my skin too raw and sore to endure even my own touch.

Cranking off the faucet, I put my palms against the tiled wall and take deep breaths in and out. I should feel better by now, but I don't. I think I feel even worse than before.

A simple touch from the girl I'm infatuated with sent me off the fucking deep end. I've never been able to stand being touched since I was a kid and all the bad things happened to me. My brain associates touch and love with pain and torment, and rightly so given my fucked-up childhood.

I had a lot of people hurt me in my past. I'm mentally and physically fucking scarred, and there is nothing in the world that can ever erase the suffering I endured as a scared, little boy.

The last thing I wanted was for Adeline to see me like this. More than anything, I'm embarrassed that she witnessed me in that fucked-up mental state once again.

After my breathing calms down and my heart stops threatening to beat out of my chest, I climb out of the shower and dry off. Then I grab the clothes from the floor and neatly fold them before placing them in the empty dirty clothes bin.

I hang up my towel on a drying rack before going to my closet for something to wear. I pull a simple, dark Henley shirt over my head and then slip into a pair of black boxer briefs and black lounge pants.

I hardly ever dress so casual, but I'm not feeling like my usual fucked-up self at the moment. I suffered a major panic attack, and thinking about facing Adeline again makes me sick to my stomach.

Retreating into the bathroom once more, I go through my regular after-shower routine of brushing my teeth and rinsing with mouthwash, putting on two different kinds of deodorant under my arms, styling my hair until every single hair is in its perfect place and then washing my hands seven times with antibacterial soap.

As I'm drying my hands, I stare at my reflection in the large mirror. A grimace appears on my face, and I shake my head. I'm fucking disgusted with myself and the way I acted.

It's not like it's the first time someone has touched me when I didn't want them to, but I sure as hell never lost my shit like I did tonight.

Why did her touch bother me so much even though I've been foolishly yearning for it since she arrived on the island? Why is *everything* so different with her?

Am I secretly hoping that there could be something more between us than just what I purchased from her?

No.

I shoot that idea down right away. I'm incapable of having more of a relationship with her…or anyone, for that matter. No. Adeline simply caught me off guard. I have to convince myself that that's all there is to it. *Nothing more.*

* * * * * * *

LATER THAT NIGHT, when I know she's in bed, I sneak into Adeline's room and watch her sleep.

She looks like an angel lying there surrounded by the white sheets, her thick, dark lashes dusting her delicate cheekbones and her long hair draped over the pillows. Her chest gently rises and falls, and the rhythmic sound of her deep, even breaths somehow soothes my dark soul.

She's so fucking beautiful that it hurts to look at her, like staring into the sun.

I move closer to the bed just as her delicate brows furrow and her breathing picks up.

And then I hear my name on her lips.

"Lucien," she whispers before a sharp gasp.

For a moment I think she's awake and saw me watching her sleep, but her eyes remain closed. She's having a dream…or perhaps a nightmare.

My hand automatically reaches for her, but I stop short of touching her. Instead, I hush her and tell her that everything's going to be okay.

Eventually, Adeline's features smooth out, and she relaxes once more into a deep sleep. She doesn't utter my name again, and I'm glad for that.

Taking one last lingering gaze at the sleeping beauty, I quietly leave her room.

Even though Adeline may look like she just stepped out of a fairytale, I can't let myself believe that I'm her Prince Charming.

I'm nothing more than the dark villain in her story.

And my black soul can never be redeemed.

CHAPTER 17

ADELINE

THIS IS CRAZY.

I keep repeating those words over and over again in my brain. They ricochet off the sides of my skull and come back like a boomerang.

I'm making the finishing touches on the makeup I borrowed from Maria, and then I stand back from the mirror to admire the final product.

My eyes are smoky and alluring. My lips are brushed with a glossy pink lipstick. My body is covered in a black and green lace chemise complete with matching thong, and black stockings. And my long, chestnut-brown hair is falling down my shoulders and back in soft waves.

I don't look like myself. I look like another person entirely. And that feeling of taking on another persona is the only thing that's going to get me through tonight. I have to detach and become someone else, or I'll never make it out of here mentally intact.

I slowly skim my hands down the length of my body. I'm trembling with anticipation…mixed in with a little bit of fear.

Tonight is the night.

I made the unconscionable decision days ago that I'm going to finally give in to Lucien.

Things have been strained between us ever since the other night when Lucien freaked out when I touched him, but I'm hoping that this outfit will change his mind.

I can't keep on living here in this life with my captor, who flies off the handle at any given moment. How long before he hurts me…or kills me?

He promised to let me go if I gave him what he wants. And my virginity is not worth an eternity in this monotonous hell. The solitude and utter lack of stimulation from the outside world have been driving me insane. I would rather just get this whole thing over with and deal with the consequences to my mental state later if it means getting to go home.

I've come to terms with the fact that Lucien's not going to rape me. In fact, he hasn't laid a single finger on me since I arrived…but I think that might have more to do with his strange affliction to being touched. He told me I had to come to him willingly, and I finally feel like I'm ready. I just hope I can convince him of that.

In less than twenty-four hours, I could be on my way to see Giovanni again. In my dreams, I picture him distraught from not being able to find me and welcoming me home with open arms.

But in my nightmares, I come home to a disgruntled father and a devastated fiancé. What if they blame me for what happened to me? What if Gio never truly forgives me?

No.

I refuse to think like that any longer.

The sooner you give me what I want, the sooner you can leave.

I stare at my reflection one last time and whisper to myself, "You can do this."

It's amazing what solitude can do to a person. I have spent the better part of the day reevaluating my life.

I always thought my father was protecting me from all the evils in the world and that I was one of the luckiest girls on the planet. I'm beginning to think the exact opposite now. And the more I dwell on it, the angrier I become. I'm starting to finally see my life differently and not through the rose-colored glasses I once wore.

My father was abusive. I've never put the way he punished me in such a harsh way before, but when I think back to the many times he beat me with a belt for the smallest transgression, yes, I think abuse is the perfect way to describe it now.

Sometimes I think he just needed to take his anger out on someone. My sisters once told me our father blamed me for our mother's death. I never believed it…or maybe I never wanted to believe it. But now I think it's true.

My mother had a lot of complications during the delivery. She passed away soon after I was born, and I never had the chance to meet her. I like to think that had she never died, my life would be completely different. But maybe she lived under my father's thumb as well…and maybe nothing would have changed.

I saw Giovanni as a savior, but didn't truly know the reason why I felt that way. I was stuck in denial. Denial of my father's treatment towards me and denial of how desolate my life truly was.

Take away the fancy clothes and charity events, and you're left with a girl who had the weight on her shoulders to perform and to be perfect. And very much like a bird with its wings clipped, so that it can't fly away, I too was put in a cage and locked away.

I used to think all of that was normal, but maybe it's because it's the only way I truly ever knew how to live. I never had any friends….unless you consider a nanny or tutor a friend.

I was never allowed outside to explore on my own, constantly surrounded by bodyguards and security. I never even kissed a boy or held hands before my father suddenly thrust Giovanni into my life. And once again, the choice of who I could marry was taken away as well.

I think in time I could have grown to love Giovanni. He would have taken care of me, and I think he was fond of me as well. But now I'm not feeling too sure about that either.

This isolation has put everything in my life into a different perspective, and I feel myself slowly crumbling away. I've never felt so dejected before in my entire life. At least I was happy in my naïve little bubble before I came here. But now I'm starting to wonder if I even want to return home if I can escape from this place. Could I possibly start over, make a life for myself, a life that I want and make choices that I choose? Is that even possible? If my father thinks I'm dead…maybe it is.

Tonight, I shall suffer with Lucien, but tomorrow I will be a free woman. And if he really does give me the million dollars, I won't even have to return to New York right away.

Maybe I'll go somewhere and start a new life, a place where I can choose who I want to marry. A place where I can be whoever and whatever I want.

Then I won't have to worry or face the consequences of what happened to me. I won't have to face my father or Giovanni until I so choose.

And I won't have to see the look of disgust on their faces when I tell them what I did in exchange for my freedom.

Tears fill my green eyes, but I quickly blink them away. "No time for crying now," I tell my reflection in the mirror. "You're on a mission."

I'm going to seduce Lucien tonight.

CHAPTER 18

LUCIEN

I CAN SENSE a change in her the moment I enter the room. Earlier, I'd watched her on the camera feed picking out a sexy outfit to wear, perfecting her hair and makeup in the bathroom and then concealing the lingerie under a silk robe before I came to her bedroom for dinner.

As we eat, I have to fight to keep a smirk off of my face. My little captive is ready to play, and I couldn't be happier. After waiting a week for her to come around, I'd almost grown bored of our situation.

I'm hoping once she finally agrees to give me what I want, I can send her on her way and never think of her again.

She's definitely become more than just an obsession to me.

She's become an unwanted distraction.

Even though it's been nice to suppress most of my dark thoughts when I'm around her, I haven't been myself. And that's scaring the shit out of me. I mean, I watched her sleep the other night for fuck's sake. That's not me. That's not who or what I am. And Adeline makes me forget who I am.

Not that that's a bad thing sometimes. But I *need* control. I *need* order.

And she makes me feel reckless and helpless all at the same time. If only she knew how much power she actually holds over me...

Adeline picks at her dinner, barely eating more than a few bites. I know she's nervous and anxious, but the bastard in me refuses to give in and make things easy on her. So, I take my time eating, even though I can't even taste a damn thing. My mind is on overdrive thinking about all the things I want to do to her tonight.

She's made me wait so long, and I intend to draw this out for as long as possible. Besides, she might be the last one before I bring the Valenti empire to the ground. I may as well enjoy my last taste of the forbidden fruit while I still can.

Adeline picks up her wine glass, her hand trembling at first until she forces it steady. I act like I don't notice, but I notice everything about her. Every. Single. Thing.

She doesn't sip the wine. She practically gulps it down. And while that would normally make me nauseous, it only adds more fuel to the fire stoking inside of me.

I want to make her fear me. I want to make her tremble under me when I shove my cock into her soft, tight cunt for the first time.

I don't ever remember wanting anything more than her. And I'm practically salivating over the thought of taking her and making her mine.

Wrapping my fingers around my own wine glass, I take a few sips to calm the beast trying to take forefront in my mind. I need to bide my time. Let her come to me. And then, once she lets her guard down, I'll strike like a predator lying in wait.

"Enjoying the wine?" I ask her when she polishes off her glass in no time at all, not even allowing herself to enjoy the taste of the expensive and vintage burgundy.

She holds her fingers up to her lips to cover a shy smile. "Yes. Sorry." She places her glass back on the table. "I know you don't like that," she adds in a whisper.

Inclining my head, I stare at her in interest. Maybe I've gotten it all wrong. Maybe I'm not the only one studying the other's every move.

She's acting like she's gotten to know me in our short time together, but she couldn't be more wrong. She's only scratched the surface to my deviance.

I watch her closely as she picks up a strawberry, dips it in whipped cream and brings it to her mouth. Her pink tongue slides out between her full lips to lick at the white cream, and I can barely contain the groan threatening to escape my throat.

She's doing all of this on purpose to entice and tease me.

And, fuck, she's doing a great job at it.

My eyes track the movement of her tongue. I'm completely enamored as her lips part and her perfectly straight, white teeth sink their way into the flesh of the strawberry.

I'm practically squirming in my seat even though this is not how this game is supposed to be playing out. I'm supposed to be the one making her squirm, not the other way around.

Forcing my attention away from her, I pick up my own strawberry and bite into it. It's juicy and sweet, and now I can imagine her lips tasting the same.

Fuck. Me.

I close my eyes and try to focus on other things, but it proves to be nearly impossible. When I open them back up, Adeline is staring at me with a come-hither look from across the table.

I make no movement to go to her, demanding control of this situation even if I've never felt more out of control than this exact moment. After a few seconds of tension-filled silence, I watch, frozen in my chair, as she slowly stands and reaches for the sash of her robe. With only a brief hesitation, she undoes the bow and slips out of the robe, the silky material whispering as it falls to the floor behind her.

My eyes greedily peruse her gorgeous body wrapped up in black and green lace and her legs covered in black stockings. "Fuck, you're beautiful,"

I whisper the compliment and am surprised when she gives me a shy smile and a subtle shade of pink creeps across her cheeks.

I stay seated, allowing her to run the show…at least for now. I need her to feel confident and safe and in control even though it won't last long, unfortunately, for her.

Adeline takes a few steps towards me, her luscious tits practically pouring out over the top of the lingerie. She looks like a special, sexy package that I want to unwrap. "I want you to strip for me," I tell her in a demanding whisper. "Slowly."

As she stands before me, I can practically feel the edginess and fear coming off of her in waves.

And it turns me the fuck on.

She rolls the stockings down her long legs, and I watch her, mesmerized by her every movement. I've never had a woman captivate me so much as Adeline has. I know I should be worried by the alarm bells going off in my head that this is going to end badly for me, but I ignore them and continue with this dangerous game I've been playing with this gorgeous creature.

When she slowly pulls the chemise up over her taut, lithe body, my growing erection presses painfully against the zipper of my pants. I welcome the biting pain, though, because it distracts my inner beast from taking over.

I don't want to scare her…just yet.

The chemise drops to the floor, and Adeline's hands modestly cover her breasts as she stares at me with apprehension lacing her features. She's standing naked before me in only a thong, her delicate throat working over a nervous swallow.

Standing from my chair, I slowly saunter over to her. I stop behind her, towering over her small, petite frame, and I can feel the nervousness practically coming off of her in waves. She seemed so damn confident when I first entered the room, but now she's trembling. I need to warm her up to the idea of me taking her tonight, and I know just the way.

Steeling myself, I inhale a deep breath before releasing it while I try to mentally prepare for what's about to happen. I don't like to touch the women I buy, but, unfortunately, some contact is necessary in order for me to get what I want.

I absolutely abhor being touched, a fear that stems from my fucked-up childhood. But as long as I remain in control of what's happening to me, I can tolerate some things.

"Hands at your sides, fingertips touching your thighs," I instruct her, my breath skating over the shell of her ear. Once she's done as I've said, I tell her, "Don't move. Understand?"

After I get a nod of compliance, I step behind Adeline, my hands shaking as I reach for her. I force them steady as my hands skim over her hips and move up to cup her breasts. I hiss out an unsteady breath. They fit my palms perfectly, and they feel soft, like silk.

"Fuck. You're perfect," I breathe against her nape, and it causes a shiver to run through her.

I pinch Adeline's pretty, pink nipples between my finger and thumb, rolling them gently until she releases a whimper. Her fingertips twitch against her thighs as I snake my right hand down her flat, toned stomach and under the material of her thong. When the pads of my fingers touch her smooth mound, I almost combust right on the spot.

She shaved for me. And knowing that she took the extra care to please me makes me hard as fuck.

"Perfect," I whisper in her ear, and I'm rewarded with another tremor that makes my dick pulse and strain against the fine wool of my dress pants.

When my fingertip traces the length of her slit and I find her slick and ready for me, my breath catches in my throat. Adeline's already turned on by this, and I've just gotten started.

Oh, this is going to be fun, I think to myself.

She's responsive. *Really responsive.* And once again, she manages to surprise me.

My fingertip finds her swollen, little nub, and I rub her gently. She inhales sharply, her head falling back against my shoulder. Her lips are only a few inches away from my jaw, and I can feel her sharp pants against my neck.

Normally, all this skin-to-skin contact would have me overwhelmed and on the verge of panic, but all I can think about in this moment is Adeline and how much I want to make her feel good before I take what's mine.

Sexy, little moans erupt from her full lips as I caress her clit with my fingertips. Her fingernails dig into the flesh of her thighs, and I know she's struggling with my demands not to touch me.

A small moan escapes her lips for only a moment, before she slams her jaw shut, muffling the sound. My free hand immediately wraps around her throat, holding her head against my chest as her back arches. "I want to hear you," I hiss into her hair that smells divine, like a ripe peach.

I can feel her pulse thundering under the pad of my thumb as my fingers strum her like a finely tuned instrument. Her mouth opens on its own volition, and this time she can't contain the almost scream erupting from her throat.

Fuck.

My hand tightens around her throat, but not to the point of hurting her. Nevertheless, a little bit of panic has her hands moving towards my hand. I immediately stop manipulating her clit, and her hands stop before she can touch me. Eventually, they return to her thighs, and I continue strumming her, wanting to elicit her beautiful moans once more.

"Good girl," I growl in her ear as her fingernails dig into her thighs again. "I want you to come for me," I demand, wanting to hear her screams more than anything I've ever wanted before.

It's not long before she tenses up and cries out, her entire body trembling against me as she comes on command. I hold her against me, keeping her upright when her knees threaten to buckle. I can't help but smirk against her hair at the powerful orgasm I just gave her.

After she calms down and her breathing returns to almost normal, I pull back from her, leaving her on unsteady legs. "Go lay on the bed," I tell her before walking over to the closet on the other side of the room. After gathering several long and colorful scarves, I come back into the room and allow myself a few moments to drink in the sight of her lying in the middle of the king-sized bed, waiting for me.

She's painfully beautiful and sexy as fuck wearing only a thong and shaking like a leaf. Long gone is the confident lioness she was when I first walked in the door. Now, she's a shy and timid, little mouse.

Her eyes widen as she catches sight of the scarves in my hands as I approach the bed. "W-what are those f-for?" she asks, her shuddering worsening.

"I need to tie you up," I state, not bothering to elaborate any more than that. I have my reasons for wanting to tie her up. I have to be the one in charge of accepting what's happening to me. I have to be in control of everything, and I can't risk her touching me when I'm not ready.

Placing the bundle of silk on the nightstand beside me, I take one, blue and yellow scarf in my hands, stretching the material and almost groaning at the thought of tying Adeline up with it. She will look so perfect trussed up in this bed. It will be a memory I will keep with me forever…long after she's gone.

But when I reach for her wrist, she snatches her hand away from me at the last second.

"Please, Lucien. Don't."

My name on her lips and her terror-filled tone catch my attention. My gaze snaps up to meet her pretty face. The undiluted fear in her gaze has me hesitating. She's staring at the scarf in my hand like it's a snake waiting to strike.

My grip tightens on the scarf in my hands, and I breathe in and out as slowly as I can. I've always tied up the girls I purchased, because I can't take the risk. None of the women before her ever had a problem with being tied up. It was all just part of the deal.

I know I should just force her to obey me. After all, I bought her. She's mine to do with whatever I please.

But at the same time, I know exactly what she's going through right now. Horrible memories of my past barrage me, and I'm barely able to contain them.

My breathing picks up and turns into sharp, harsh pants as I tighten my grip on the scarf in my hands, threatening to rip the material.

"Lucien," Adeline's voice reaches me through the darkness…a light at the end of a very dark universe.

When my eyes snap open, I gaze down at the breathtaking beauty below me.

"It's okay. You can...you can tie me up," she says, the tremor in her voice giving her away instantly.

Shaking my head, I eventually relinquish the scarf, letting it fall to the floor at my feet. Angry with myself for not taking the control I need, I motion to her hands and demand, "Keep your hands wrapped around the bedframe." When she gives me several quick nods, I add vehemently, "Don't you *dare* move them."

Watching her small hands wrap around the metal bars doesn't make me feel the least bit better, though, and I realize it's because a part of me wants to know what it would feel like to have her hands on me. Her fingers spearing through my dark hair, pulling my face down close to hers. Our lips locking in a searing kiss...something I've never allowed myself to partake in before.

Shaking my head and pushing the crazy notion aside, I force myself to focus on the here and now instead of what could and what will *never* be.

Adeline's thickly lashed, sparkling, emerald eyes blink up at me. The innocent doe-eyed look on her face does weird things to me, making me feel things I don't want to feel right now, and so I focus on her body instead.

Sitting down on the edge of the bed, leaving about an inch of space between us, my hands tremble as I reach out and stroke her quivering, flat stomach, which feels like the softest silk imaginable. I stifle a groan as I gently trace my hands across her skin.

Knowing that she took a two hour and thirty-three minute shower not long before dinner keeps my demon at bay.

She's clean, I repeatedly tell myself in my head.

The need to be in control begins to override everything else as my hands make their way to the apex of her thighs.

I made her leave the thong on, and she looks like a delicious present I want to unwrap. My fingertips hook into the lace and slowly pull it away and down her legs, unveiling her pretty, pink pussy.

I discard the lace at the edge of the bed and turn my attention back to her. Carefully, I spread apart her smooth, pink lips with my fingertips and stare at her gorgeous little clit. When I run my finger over the little button, Adeline jumps and stares down at me with wide eyes. She squirms under my ministrations, clearly uncomfortable with having me so up close and personal.

My gaze meets hers as I ask her the question I've been dying to ask, even though I don't know if I want to know the answer. "How many men have touched you down here?"

Her teeth sink into her bottom lip, and her wavering gaze has me fearing the worst. But when she says, "Just you," I breathe a sigh of relief.

She could be lying to me, but I don't see deceit in her gaze. I see embarrassment at me being the first...the man who bought her.

"How many orgasms have you had?" I ask, wanting --- no, *needing* to know.

Her eyes squeeze shut, blocking me out. She doesn't want to open up to me, but I know just how to make her talk. Stroking my fingertips up and down her slit, her eyes snap open and her lips part on a gasp.

"How many?" I ask again, more forcefully this time.

"One...the one you gave me," she confesses.

Her answer has my cock growing as hard as steel. "Fuck, Adeline. I want to be your first for everything," I confess to her before I can stop myself.

Her eyes widen at my confession, but she doesn't utter a word. It's probably better that way for both of us after my idiotic slip-up.

Adeline's time here is limited. After tonight, she'll be nothing but a distant memory. And I shouldn't have to remind myself of that fact. She's the seventh one that I purchased for my sick obsession. And once I'm done with her, she'll disappear like all the others before her.

Forcing my attention back to her pretty pussy, I continue to finger her until she's gyrating against my hand on her own volition and gasping out the most melodic noises I've ever heard.

After the second orgasm rips through her and she comes back down from it, there's a noticeable change in her demeanor. She seems calmer now, more relaxed with hooded eyes and the ghost of a smile touching her lips.

I realize she was probably thinking I was going to just force my way inside, ripping through her virginity without an ounce of foreplay. But this isn't how this game works. I want her nice and wet and relaxed when I take her for the first time.

I want her to want this between us…and want me.

Standing, I slowly unbutton my dress shirt, fold it and place it on a nearby chair. I retrieve a condom from the pocket of my dress pants before I strip out of them along with my boxer briefs, meticulously folding them as well before placing them on top of my shirt.

Naked, I stroll back over to the bed and watch as Adeline's eyes greedily drink me in. I spend a lot of time working out to achieve my sculpted body, and I like knowing that she's admiring it. I have numerous scars on my back that she can't see, and I intend to keep it that way.

I don't want to ruin her reverence with the ugly truth of my past.

Her eyes are glued to my heavy, hard cock between my legs, and I almost chuckle at her blatant curiosity. Maintaining a stoic expression, I climb on the bed beside her. Her pink tongue sneaks out past her lips and runs along her lips. I'm entranced by the simple movement as I move between her thighs.

I fist my hard cock, pumping several times and watching her watch me with wide eyes. I rip through the gold foil packet and place the wrapper neatly on the edge of the nightstand before rolling the condom down my length.

Our eye contact is unwavering as I press the head of my cock against her slick entrance. Her smooth, silky thighs involuntarily squeeze against mine, and I breathe through the panic that threatens to rise through me.

Adeline opens her mouth as if she wants to say something, maybe tell me to stop, as if she has a choice right now, but she quickly closes it again, staring into my eyes with trepidation but also…trust. She's trusting me not to hurt her.

A sick part of me wants to hurt her just to make her realize that the world is full of monsters and that you can't truly trust anyone. I know that better than anyone.

But having been on the receiving end of enough pain to last three lifetimes, I could never actually hurt this girl the way I've been hurt.

Gripping my cock in one hand and holding my weight up with the other hand placed by her head, I guide myself inch by delicious inch inside of her tight, virgin cunt.

When I break past the barrier of her virginity for the first time, Adeline gasps, and her hands suddenly move from the wrought iron bars as she places her small palms on my chest to either slow me or stop me altogether, but I'm too far gone. I sink as deep as I can, knowing the pain for her will only be temporary.

Adeline's eyes grow large, and she inhales sharply once I'm completely rooted inside of her. Her silky walls are gripping me so tightly, and I have to force myself not to move, to give her time to adjust to me.

When her fingertips twitch against my hard chest, that's when I realize she's been touching me ever since I first entered her. I know I should tell her to put her hands back on the bars. I should remind her of the *rules*.

But fuck the rules. Her touch, for the first time in my life, feels fucking good, and I welcome it despite my typical aversion, despite my fears.

Withdrawing from her slowly, I thrust back in right away. She lets out a noise that's a mixture of a moan and a cry, and it makes my dick turn to steel, fueling the desire raging inside of me.

Growling low in the back of my throat, I pull back and thrust into her hard once more. Her pussy grips me like a vice in response, giving me a taste of what can only be described as heaven.

Her eyes slowly open and lock onto mine, but I shudder under the intensity of her gaze. Shaking my head, I stare down at the crisp, white sheet beside her chestnut locks. Those emerald green orbs have been haunting my dreams at night, and I can't afford to forge any kind of connection with her. Not now. Not like this.

But when I begin thrusting in and out of her and she releases the most primal and melodious noises I've ever heard in my life, my attention snaps right back to her beautiful face, etched in ecstasy. Our eyes meet again, and I become locked in some sort of trance, not willing to break it again.

With her gaze holding me hostage, I draw my cock out of her tight, wet pussy and sink back into her. The action makes her eyes drift almost completely closed, threatening to break the spell she clearly has me under. But she continues to stare up at me…as if I'm her whole world in that moment.

Pistoning my hips, I begin a torturous rhythm that has her hands moving from my chest to my shoulders as she quivers under me. Her touch is driving me insane, but I can't seem to force myself to tell her to stop.

Her head thrashes from side to side on the bed as she sinks her teeth down into her bottom lip, not allowing herself to voice any more sounds of pleasure. She's denying the pleasure her traitorous body is trying to partake in. And it makes me work even harder for her orgasm. I want to hear her cries.

I want to hear her scream my fucking name.

I stare down at Adeline in awe as I withdraw almost completely, before thrusting home again. And then I repeat the maneuver, wanting to feel her come around my cock while I'm seated deep within her tight walls.

Her powerful orgasm erupts out of nowhere, and her mouth opens on a silent scream. I fuck Adeline faster and faster, drawing out the pleasure until she's a mumbling, quivering mess under me.

Cupping her round ass in my hands, I tilt her hips up and drive into her with a punishing rhythm, relishing in the fact that I must be hitting just the right spot inside of her when her breath catches and her nails bite into my shoulders.

That type of touch and pain would normally have me freaking out, but my brain is not concentrating on germs or touch or any of the other normal fucked-up things. I can only see and breathe and feel Adeline, and the feeling is exquisite. She's like some kind of magic cure for all my ailments in this moment.

Her velvety folds clench around my shaft, and her full lips part on a groan as her walls begin to spasm, gripping me so goddamn tight. I pick up my pace and thrust into her over and over again, hitting that magic spot inside of her as she begins to whimper and then cries out as another orgasm wracks her lithe body underneath me.

I'm counting the orgasms she's had in my head, and suddenly I want to find out how many more I can strum out of her. For the first time ever, I want *more*. So much more.

Burying myself into her, I force my pace to slow, because I don't want this to end. I want to draw this out for as long as fucking possible. Never before did I want something to last forever until now.

"Please," Adeline begs through soft pants.

I don't know whether she's asking me for more or asking me to stop. Probably the latter, but she's not in charge here, even of her own body.

I am.

"More," I demand as I stare into her beautiful, sparkling, green eyes.

Her lips quiver as she releases a shuddering breath, and I can feel her pussy gripping me tightly before spasming out of control. Her back bows off the bed, and she cries out louder than before. It's like my dick was made just for her tight cunt --- a perfect fit. And the fact that she's so responsive to me only makes me want her more.

My balls slap against her soaking wet pussy as I fuck her deeply, drawing out the pleasure from her. When she comes down from the high, I bring my weight down to my elbows, our bodies now so close that I can feel her sharp pants on my lips. Her breath smells sweet like mint and strawberries, the dessert we shared at dinner.

Her stare jumps from my eyes to my lips and back again. She wants me to kiss her, and the strong urge to give in hits me hard. But that is one step I'm not willing to take with Adeline.

The shock from how different this time with Adeline is from all the other girls is almost overwhelming. Usually, I'm rough, detached, taking what I want and leaving just as quickly as I arrived. My needs are usually squelched as soon as I push past their innocence, and then the rest is just a blur...mechanical...cold. Their pleasure never concerned me.

But with Adeline, this is all new and unexpected.

And I have no idea why.

When I feel Adeline's hands moving to my back, the feel of her fingernails lightly scraping down my skin and over my scars does something to me. Instead of freaking out or pulling away from her, I allow her to continue to touch me. I can't seem to tell her no or demand she not do it. Instead, it's almost like I want her to.

Hesitantly, I wrap my arms around her, pressing and holding her deliciously naked body against mine. And this suddenly feels...real...*too real*. It's as if the circumstances of our situation no longer exist. We're just a normal couple making love for the first time, and nothing else and no one else in the world fucking matters.

"Fuck, Adeline," I growl against her neck, no longer being able to tell which way is up. I'm so fucking confused and blissed out of my mind on her. She's like a drug that I can't stop craving more of.

I slowly and methodically piston my hips against her over and over again; my entire body feeling like it's on fire. I'm so close, so fucking close. But I want to feel her come one last time.

When I feel her tight walls gripping me like a glove and the needy rocking of her hips, I know she's close too. I pull back a few inches to look at her devastatingly beautiful face, and our gazes stay locked as I drag one last orgasm from her. Adeline clutches to me as if I'm her lifeline, her body flush with mine as she shudders and cries out my fucking name.

Hearing my name mixed in with her moans drives me over the edge.

The last waves of her orgasm clench around my length, milking my cock as bright, hot pleasure crashes over me, sending burning sparks down my spine. I come with a shout, thrusting erratically into her three more times before completely stilling inside of her.

Groaning, I close my eyes and lick my lips. My arms shake as I struggle to hold my weight off of her. I've never come so hard in my entire life, and the feeling is euphoric, almost surreal.

I open my eyes and stare down at her green orbs, which are studying me. I take in every feature of her beautiful face, etching it into my memory. Our time together is almost up, and I desperately want to remember this moment forever.

The thought of not having her again almost guts me.

And it's in that moment that I realize for the first time ever...I don't want to let her go.

CHAPTER 19

ADELINE

I STARE UP at Lucien as he hovers over me, breathing harshly. His eyes are transfixed on me as I quake underneath him from the aftershocks of what felt like my millionth orgasm. Groaning, he closes his eyes and licks his full lips that I suddenly want to kiss.

What just happened between us is indescribable. I wouldn't be able to describe it even if I wanted to. Something shifted between us, and he became so much more than my captor.

He became my lover.

And for one miniscule second, I allowed myself to play into the fantasy, holding onto him like I never wanted to let go of the dream.

My euphoria is short lived, however, because Lucien's warm gaze suddenly grows icy, and the ever-present scowl that I've become used to appears on his face once more. Without so much as a word or a caressing touch, he pulls out of me, leaving me feeling cold and confused.

He tosses the condom into a small trashcan by the nightstand and begins to quickly get dressed. Mumbling to himself, I can see the emotions as they play out on his face.

Satisfaction…confusion…apprehension…and…*regret*.

The last one hits me hard as his dark gaze finally meets mine. A few minutes ago, he was making love to me like I was the most precious thing in the world to him.

But now…now it's almost as if he's looking through me. Like I don't exist. Like I'm some discarded, little plaything.

Hastily, I wrap the sheets around my nudity, suddenly feeling very vulnerable and exposed.

Lucien reaches into his pants pocket for a bottle I instantly recognize. He squirts a large amount of the sanitizer all over his palm before hurriedly scrubbing his fingers, hands, wrists and muscular forearms.

Tears fill my eyes as I watch his ritual. *Does he think I'm…dirty? Is he disgusted by me?*

I can't stop the self-deprecating questions from bombarding my mind. And then I quickly tell myself I don't care. I shouldn't care. Not about this. Certainly not about him.

Lucien let me touch him even though I told him I wouldn't. Keeping my hands on the bedframe proved to be more than difficult when he tore through my virginity. The pain was sharp, but, thankfully, quick. And before I knew it, my hands were roaming all over his sculpted chest, arms and shoulders.

When I moved my hands to his muscular back, however, I felt numerous scars marring his flawless skin. I couldn't help but run my fingertips over the jagged grooves as he moved inside of me. The scars somehow made him more…human, in my mind.

This formidable, unapproachable man, who personified perfection, suddenly became flawed.

There is a reason Lucien is the way he is, and perhaps that knowledge of knowing there's a deep meaning behind all of this is keeping me from freaking out right now.

"So what happens now?" I ask, trying to keep my voice steady, but failing miserably.

"Jax will arrange everything for you to return home," he says in a cool tone, shooting me wary sidelong glances. He's detached and so much unlike how he was just a few moments ago with me.

Growing angrier by the second and feeling dejected now that the afterglow of my first time has evaporated, I ask him, "So you're going to let me go and just kidnap another girl to have sex with?" My tone is dripping with acid, and I hate that the thought of him with another woman makes me suddenly jealous.

He turns and looks at me, momentarily stopping the lathering of sanitizer on his hands.

Before he can answer me, I decide that I need to ask the question that has been in the forefront of my mind since day one.

"Why me?" I ask, and my voice is barely above a whisper. When he cocks his brow in confusion, I clarify. "Why did you choose me? Out of all the girls in the world, why did you choose *me*?"

His thick brows pinch together over his dark, intense eyes as he says, "I didn't choose you. *You* were chosen for *me*. Your handler didn't explain any of this to you?" he asks, and I can hear the frustration in his voice.

His words are not making any sense. I was chosen? By whom? And what in the hell is a handler? Someone who kidnaps poor girls off the street to sell them to rich perverts, who then in turn steal their virginity?

The way he's talking and acting…it's like I should already know all of this and what I've gotten myself into. *As if I had a choice.*

"You keep talking about a handler. Is that what you call the man who kidnapped me?" I can sense the anger starting to roll off of him in waves, but I can't seem to make myself shut up. "I don't know who chose me for you. In fact, I don't know anything about this deal you supposedly have with these people. I was kidnapped at gunpoint while I was walking home with Giovanni, my fiancé," I tell him honestly.

My words seem to visibly wound him, and he takes a step back as if their force is too much to bear. His eyes narrow for a moment before he shakes his head, a flash of irritation crossing his face. "You're lying," he hisses.

Now it's my turn to be hurt by his words, and they cut me straight to the bone. "Why would I lie about this?" I ask, my eyes shimmering with tears and blurring the man before me, who is starting to look more like a monster every second that passes. "Giovanni and I had just left a restaurant and were walking home when a group of men in ski masks showed up out of nowhere. A man with a gun grabbed me and knocked me out," I say, gently brushing past the spot on my temple that is still sore from the brunt force. "That's the last thing I remember...before waking up here."

Lucien's hands clench into fists at his sides as he glares at me. How could he be mad when he orchestrated it all?

Unless he didn't.

And then realization slowly dawns on me.

Lucien said I was chosen for him, so what if this is all one giant mistake? What if they kidnapped the wrong girl? Maybe I wasn't even supposed to be here in the first place.

Before I can say anything else, Lucien walks to the door, inputs the code and leaves, slamming the door behind him. I stare at the door for a while, expecting him to come back in, but he never does.

Tears stream down my cheeks as a sob tears from my throat. Everything that has happened in the past hour and a half hits me like a ton of bricks.

What have I done?

If this was all a mistake...then I just gave my virginity to someone who has no reason to keep me here, who might have released me once I explained to him what had happened to me.

Feeling disgusted with myself, I jump out of bed and run to the bathroom. I barely make it to the toilet in time before I'm retching and throwing up the contents of the dinner I shared with *him*.

Feeling weak and nauseated, I slowly stand up and turn the hot water knob for the shower. When I get in, the scalding water pelts my skin, but I can barely feel it. Fisting the soap in my hands, I vigorously scrub away any remnants of our time together.

When my skin is red and rubbed raw and I can no longer take the scorching water, I turn off the shower and dry off. Not bothering to dress or do my hair, I simply wrap another towel around myself, return to the bedroom and collapse onto the bed, pulling the sheet and comforter up around me and sobbing into the pillow.

What have I done?

Giovanni will *never* forgive me.

CHAPTER 20

LUCIEN

AFTER A LONG and arduous shower, which left my skin raw and bleeding, I flee to the sanctity of my office, locking myself inside.

My mind runs a million miles a minute as what Adeline confessed to me repeats over and over again in my mind like a broken fucking record.

She had told me that she'd been kidnapped at gunpoint and that she's engaged --- *fucking engaged* --- to a man named Giovanni. The name still has me reeling as I sit down in front of my computer and bring it out of sleep mode.

Scowling, I begin to pore over the notes I have on Giovanni Morello. Even though his emails are always encrypted and he attempts to cover his tracks, his offshore account to where I wired his money was easy enough to trace. Thus, providing me with a plethora of information on my supplier.

I frown when I don't find what I'm looking for in my files. I only have intricate details about his business dealings, contacts and activities, but nothing on his personal life. But then again, why would I? Why would I care about who he's fucking?

But now I'm intrigued. Now I must know everything and see if Adeline was really telling me the truth. I find it hard to believe that her fiancé is the same man who sold her, even if they do share the same first name. That idea in and of itself is so fucked up that I refuse to believe it until I see proof.

As I'm bringing up all my safeguards to keep me from being tracked by anyone while I search the web, I think back to the email Giovanni had sent me when we began this transaction. There was something that should have stuck out to me like a flashing beacon of light on dark waters in the middle of the ocean.

You will receive the goods once I receive the cash.

And I expect her to be released once you get what you paid for.

He never requested that the prior four girls be released; clearly having not given a shit what happened to the girls before Adeline. Someone must have informed him that I release the girls after I'm done with them. Perhaps one of the girls went back to Giovanni and told him what happened.

I start with the simplest of ways to garner information --- a Google search. Typing in the name Giovanni Morello and Adeline, a few hits pop up right away. Numerous photos come up under the images tab, photos that were taken at some kind of charity event. And when I see her last name in one of the captions, alarm bells start going off in my head.

Valenti.

Adeline is the youngest daughter of Salvatore Valenti, the mafia king of the east coast and the man I'm planning on taking down with a vengeance. As I change my search criteria and add the last name Valenti, my worst fears come true --- Adeline is engaged to her father's right-hand man, Giovanni Morello.

The bastard sold me his fiancé.

I sit back in my chair, trying to make sense of it all. What in the fuck would possess Giovanni to sell his boss's daughter to me? I'm pretty certain that Valenti would have no qualms about killing his future son-in-law if he knew the truth.

And then I begin to question all the possible motives behind selling Adeline to me. Was Adeline sent here to spy on me? Does she have a tracker on her that could lead them right to me?

Shaking my head, I think back to Adeline's confusion when she first arrived. Unless she's a trained actress or a pathological liar, there is no way on earth she knows who I am or what she's doing here. Besides, Jackson always does a thorough check for any foreign objects imbedded in the girls' bodies. And before they even get on the plane, one of my men removes any personal effects the women may have. I have too much to lose if anyone would find me, so I don't take any chances.

No. I think Adeline was kept in the dark about this whole thing, and that makes me angry. Giovanni knows the fucking rules. I want the girls to come to me willingly. I'm offering them a lot of money in return for what I want, what I need. And many girls are willing to offer me that. I've never had to take it by force.

That would make me truly a monster, just like the ones who hurt me in my past.

I search through article after article, digesting every piece of information I can on Adeline Valenti. She's a socialite, but also considered a recluse, only coming out of her white castle for social events run by her father.

Salvatore Valenti likes to put on airs frequently, and it looks to me like Adeline is more like a prized possession than his daughter. He likes to show her off and throw money around. He has so many crooked cops in his back pocket that he doesn't need to worry about the consequences of showcasing his wealth. In fact, he thrives at being able to brag.

I gather numerous pictures of her, pulling them from Facebook and various gossip magazine sites, and I stare at them for what seems like hours. Adeline is beautiful. No. She's painfully fucking gorgeous with long brown hair, jade-green eyes and a body that supermodels would envy. With a perfect smile and full, plump lips, she is a fucking wet dream, and the cameras love her.

However, the one thing that stands out the most in the photographs of Adeline is that she rarely smiles.

Judging on her expensive clothes and jewelry, her world may seem like a fairytale to most, but I have a feeling it's nothing more than a carefully crafted façade. Jackson had told me about the bruises covering her body.

Was Morello or Valenti hurting Adeline? I desperately want to find out.

The fierce need to protect her grows stronger by the minute, and I have to rein in these foreign emotions that are suddenly bombarding me.

After spending hours searching and finding everything I can about Adeline Valenti, I make copious notes about her in a Word document that I can print out and save for my files.

Her father is a scumbag. He deals in everything from drugs to guns…to the flesh trade, buying and selling women and children with no remorse for his actions. The latter is why I have been trying to gather enough evidence to bring his entire empire down.

I just have to wonder if Adeline knows what kind of a man her father truly is.

No. I doubt she knows her father's true dealings in the dark underbelly of society. He probably plays off his work as strictly moving money around, never revealing the true sources of his power.

Something strikes me as I glance over everything I uncovered. There are no articles about Adeline being missing. Her disappearance would most likely make headlines…or there would be some kind of inkling *somewhere*.

After more digging, I discover that Salvatore Valenti had booked a flight to California the morning of the agreed upon date that Adeline was to be brought to me.

One of the lines from Morello's email hits me hard once again.

And I expect her to be released once you get what you paid for.

What if Giovanni was desperate? And what if Adeline's father isn't aware of our dealings? Maybe this was all done without his knowledge. I do not believe that Salvatore would let his daughter be sold…especially the daughter who he clearly keeps under lock and key.

All signs are pointing to one fact --- Giovanni sold his fiancée to me, and he wants her back soon…before her father finds out she was ever missing.

CHAPTER 21

LUCIEN

JACKSON WALKS INTO my office the next morning with a puzzled look on his face. He's dressed in a light blue long-sleeve shirt and dark jeans, looking bright-eyed, bushy-tailed and all that crap --- the exact opposite of me.

"You look like shit," he tells me, never one to pull any punches. "Did you sleep at all last night?"

I shake my head solemnly. After I learned the truth about my little captive, I couldn't shut my brain off long enough to even get a wink of sleep.

And as if not sleeping wasn't enough punishment, I ambled into the state-of-the-art gym on the first floor and ran for hours on the treadmill, my feet pounding away until my mind and body were devoid of anything but pain and exertion.

Jax shifts from one foot to the other nervously. I'm sure he has a lot of questions on his mind, but he's not going to ask them. He knows better. Instead, he says, "You didn't say anything about getting the plane ready today."

I simply shrug, not really wanting to talk about the inner conflict I'm having about sending Adeline away.

"Well, you slept with her last night, so ---."

I narrow my eyes at him. "How do you know we slept together?" I demand.

"Luc, relax. My bedroom is right down the hall. I could hear…everything," he says with a knowing smirk.

The fact that my cousin was privy to hearing Adeline's pleasure-filled cries angers me beyond belief. I stand, my hands curling into fists. "From your room…or from right outside the door?" I ask him calmly even though I'm anything but calm right now.

It wouldn't be the first time Jax has overstepped his boundaries and been a voyeur.

It's kind of his thing.

He stares down at the floor, and I immediately know the answer. Swiping a hand down my face, I shake my head and say, "I would tell you that you have a serious problem, but we both know who the more fucked-up man in the room is." I flash him a sardonic smile. "Your…*fetish* is nothing compared to what I'm dealing with up here," I say while tapping on my temple.

He chuckles and glances up at me again. "Sorry, Luc. It's just…she's so…oh, wow, her voice…damn, how many times did you make her come last night? I personally lost track of ---."

His words fuel the fire enough to cause an explosion of anger within me. Before he can even finish talking, I have him pushed up against the wall, my forearm pressed against his throat. "You're overstepping again, Jax," I hiss at him through gritted teeth.

His fingers pry at the long sleeve of my shirt as he chokes out, "Okay! Okay! I'm sorry!"

I release him, and he bends over, sucking in air and coughing.

"Jesus. You never cared before."

And he's right. I never did. It's not like this is the first time I've caught Jax listening in on me with one of my girls.

But Adeline isn't just a number to me. She's special.

"She's different, though, isn't she?" Jax asks as if he had just been reading my damn thoughts. "You're possessive over her. More than you've ever been before. Hell, maybe for the first time ever."

I simply shrug at his comment, neither affirming nor denying. Frankly, it's none of his damn business.

"So tell me why you're not sending her packing then. They always leave the morning after, Luc. *Always*."

I close my eyes for a second and pinch the bridge of my nose. I didn't want to share this information with anyone, let alone Jax, but I know he won't let up until I do. "She's not safe."

"And you know this how?"

"Last night after we..." I let my voice trail off, because I still feel a tinge of guilt for sleeping with Adeline, who, unbeknownst to me, is clearly here against her will. "Adeline told me that she's engaged."

"She's *what*?" Jax practically yells.

I glare at him. "She also told me that she was kidnapped, knocked unconscious by the gunman. Stolen right off the fucking streets."

"Holy shit," he breathes, slowly absorbing all of this new information. "That explains the nasty bruise on her temple," Jax confirms.

I nod. "I spent all night researching her and her family. She's Salvatore Valenti's youngest daughter."

The mere mention of that name has Jax straightening his spine and his eyes widening. He knows the FBI has been wanting me to take down the Valenti empire for a long time now. I've been slowly building my case against the entire clan, wanting to ensure that no one goes free and that they get the max time for their crimes.

What the FBI doesn't know is that I've been buying willing girls from someone in that said empire.

Well, willing…until *now*.

I have a long list of bad guys, and I've been ticking them off slowly one by one. In exchange for my help, the U.S. government looks the other way on some of my illegal extracurricular activities on the dark web and how I make most of my money.

"Giovanni Morello, Adeline's fiancé, is the one who sold her to me. Conveniently, it was at the same time her father was going to be across the country for a few weeks. I think Morello set up the kidnapping to cover his own ass in case Valenti came to find out." I tell Jax and brace for my words to floor him.

I'm not disappointed. Jax is rendered speechless for a very long time, which is so unlike him. Jax is the complete opposite of speechless on any normal given day.

I myself had trouble grasping the concept of why a man, who clearly has everything in the world, would want to give it up. My only conclusion is that Giovanni Morello needed the money. *Badly*.

Money *is* the root of all evil, after all.

And I know that better than most, unfortunately.

"Does Adeline know all of this?" he asks quietly.

"No. And I don't plan on telling her anytime soon." I sigh and shake my head. "I can't let her go knowing she's in danger. What if he sells her again?" That question has bothered me more than I'd like to admit. If he was willing to sell her once, he could do it again…multiple times. What's stopping him? If Salvatore Valenti couldn't stop him, I don't think anyone could.

"So you need more time, more information. Is that it?"

"Yes," I say, but I'm not being totally honest. The fact of the matter is I have all the information I need to bring down her fiancé or, hell, to even have him killed. But I don't want to bring down the Valenti empire.

Not yet anyway.

I know I should return Adeline without giving two fucks about whether she'll be safe or not. After she leaves here, she's no longer my problem.

But the sick, twisted side of me wants to keep her.

I want...*more.*

This woman does something to me that I can't explain. And the thought of letting her go feels like someone is taking a knife straight to the black, deep cavity of where my heart would be beating...if I even have one. I always thought I didn't. It was so much easier to be cold, closed off and detached from the world around me and everyone in it.

But Adeline is different. She makes me *feel.* And as terrified as I am to find out what more I can gain from our fucked-up relationship in this even more than fucked-up situation, I can't let her go. She's like a powerful drug...and I am hopelessly and desperately addicted to her.

I tell Jax none of this. I need him to believe that she's in danger. I can't possibly let him know the crazy ideas swirling in my head about keeping her, about not wanting to let her go...*ever*, and certainly not about wanting her over and over again, which breaks all of the rules.

"I can't let her go until I know she's safe," I tell him, the half-truth slipping out easily.

Jax gives me a nod in agreement. "Then we'll just extend her stay for a while," he says quietly. "When are you going to tell her?"

"Tonight. At dinner."

"I'll be there," Jax says before standing and walking out of my office.

I don't stop him and I don't tell him I don't want him there, because the truth of the matter is I need his support.

Adeline has a way of ripping me to shreds with a single look.

And if I know her as well as I think I do already...

She's going to hate me when I tell her that I'm keeping her.

CHAPTER 22

ADELINE

THE NEXT MORNING I wake up completely exhausted even though I slept like the dead. After crying myself to sleep, I drifted off into a deep slumber, too tired to even dwell on all the revelations swirling in my brain that came to light after Lucien took my virginity.

My legs feel like jelly as I make my way to the adjacent bathroom. I relieve myself, wash my hands and brush my teeth. Even though it seems really early since I'm so tired, I'm sure it's almost noon based on the amount of sun that was shining through the skylights when I woke up.

So much has happened over the past week or so that it almost seems like one, big blur.

That man…my captor…he didn't just take my innocence last night. He made love to me. I had so many orgasms that I lost count. And I'm not completely sure how I feel about that.

I gave myself to him willingly, and he played my traitorous body like an instrument, slowly plucking pleasure out of me until I was completely and utterly exhausted.

Even though some of our lovemaking was tender, at the end of day, I am still his captive, something he purchased. There's nothing romantic about that, and no level of Stockholm syndrome could make me forget that fact.

And now that he knows I was kidnapped, it should change everything. Will he send me back home, or pay me to keep quiet about his indiscretions?

I have no idea, because, in all honesty, I don't even know who Lucien is. I'm starting to get a grasp on the conundrum that is Lucien, but I feel like I haven't even scratched the deep, dark surface yet.

I take a shower and get ready for the day, slipping into a teal, vintage-style floral tea dress. Lucien had promised he would release me when he was done, so I assume I'm going home today or tomorrow, whenever he can make the arrangements.

As I'm putting on some light makeup and styling my hair, I think about what will happen next. If Lucien releases me, where will I go? New York City seems like the most likely scenario, but a part of me wants to run away and hide forever, too ashamed to face my family and fiancé.

Scowling at my reflection in the mirror, I decide to put my fate in Lucien's hands. It's not as if I have much of a choice at this point. If he sends me back to NYC, then maybe that's where I'm supposed to be. Maybe Gio will welcome me back with open arms, and we can continue where we left off.

That's what I'm hoping for anyway, but it's hard to be optimistic when I'm being held against my will on an island.

There is a small knock on the door before one of the maids enters with lunch. I run out of the bathroom and try to ask her about when I'm going home, but the young girl with big, brown eyes simply shakes her head with a confused look and leaves quietly.

Blowing out a frustrated breath, I sit down and pick my way through my grilled chicken salad, barely able to eat. I'm too worried about my future at this point, and food is the furthest thing on my mind right now.

Setting the tray aside, it's not long before the same maid comes back to collect my barely eaten meal. I don't even bother trying to talk to her, since she clearly doesn't understand a word I'm saying.

As the minutes tick by and no one else shows up, I move to the bed and sit on the edge, nervously bouncing my knee up and down as I consider my options. Unfortunately, I have none. I can't leave until Lucien says so.

Sighing, I fall back on the plush comforter and close my eyes.

It doesn't take long for sleep to pull me under once again.

* * * * * * *

MARIA COMES TO my room that evening to tell me that Lucien requests me to come downstairs and join him for dinner. Considering he's been dining in my room for the past week or so, this is definitely a nice change and hopefully a turn in the right direction.

I might be going home soon, I think to myself, smiling effortlessly as I follow Maria into the large dining hall. But the smile on my face slowly disappears as I realize that Lucien and I won't be dining alone tonight.

The tall, dark-haired American I saw in the kitchen during my escape attempt is sitting to the right of Lucien. They're both wearing dark suits, but the stranger is sans tie whereas Lucien is impeccably dressed, as usual, with a tie and even cufflinks and his hair perfectly styled.

As I hesitantly approach the two men, they are engaged in a serious conversation that ceases abruptly when I get within earshot.

Lucien looks troubled, barely meeting my eyes as he motions for me to take a seat across the table from the man with the familiar steel-gray eyes.

Swallowing hard, I take a seat, my glare never leaving the mysterious man, who I know deep down in my gut had something to do with bringing me to this godforsaken island.

To my surprise, the man flashes me a friendly smile with pearly whites and says, "Adeline, it's nice to properly meet you. My name is Jackson. I'm Lucien's cousin."

Well, that explains why the two men look somewhat similar. Jackson is very handsome with the same shade of dark brown hair, but Lucien is on a whole other tier by himself since he looks like a Greek god and is much taller and much more domineering than his cousin.

"Hello," I manage to squeak out. I'm on edge, and I ball my fidgeting hands against my thighs under the tablecloth.

Lucien motions for the first course to be served. When a bowl of some kind of cream soup is placed in front of me, my stomach rolls with indifference, too upset to even think about food right now.

Feeling two sets of intimidating and watchful eyes on me, however, I force myself to eat a few spoonfuls before placing my spoon down and drinking most of the wine in my glass. The wine, like always, tastes expensive, and it helps to settle my nerves a bit.

The second course comes shortly thereafter, and I can't even bring myself to taste the delicious-smelling baked chicken and broccoli dish.

The tension is thick in the room, so thick you could cut it with a knife. And it's only making this entire situation that much harder.

Drinking the last of my wine down for some liquid courage, I turn my attention to Lucien. "When am I going home?" I ask him, my voice just above a whisper.

He shifts in his chair and meets my gaze. "I don't know yet."

I'm taken aback by his uncertainty. Lucien seems to be the type who plans things out not just weeks in advance, but months and years. The fact that he doesn't know when he's releasing me makes me extremely nervous. However, I try to keep my voice calm as I ask, "What do you mean you don't know? You can't get the plane ready or...?" I try to think of a million excuses that he could possibly have as to why he's not letting me go.

"It's too dangerous for me to let you leave right now."

"Too dangerous," I repeat, tasting the bitter words. "My father...my father can protect me. He can ---"

"Your father can do many things, Adeline, but he can't protect you, not when it comes to this."

"You know who my father is?" I ask, my voice wavering.

"I know all about *Salvatore Valenti*," he hisses with contempt.

I gasp at my father's name coming from Lucien's lips. He knows who I am and about my family? Perhaps he's known all along. A sick feeling creeps up my spine. "You kidnapped me for ransom money, didn't you?" I spit accusingly. My eyes search his face, frantic for answers.

His brows pinch together in frustration. "Does it look like I need the money?" he asks, mockingly.

As much as his answer and attitude anger me, he's right. He would have nothing to gain other than padding his already fat pockets.

"I have contacts in the U.S. who handle and supply me with *willing* women who are paid handsomely to…give me what I want." He regards me silently for a few moments. "Someone in your father's inner circle kidnapped and sold you to me. I had no idea that had happened to you, or that someone had broken the rules, until you told me last night," he says crossly, clearly upset over the turn of events.

"I can't let you go without knowing that you'll be safe." He hesitates. "The person who betrayed you and your father could sell you again."

My hands tremble as I grasp the edge of the table to steady myself. I'm dizzy from all the knowledge my brain is attempting to process, and I'm sure the wine I pretty much chugged is not helping either.

So, all this time Lucien thought I was a willing participant who wanted to sleep with him for money. If I had told him about the kidnapping before we had sex, would he have let me go without taking what he paid for? Would I still be a virgin?

I just don't know the answers to those questions, but it's too late now anyway. What's done is done.

"Do you understand what I'm telling you, Adeline?" Lucien asks after I'm quiet for a long time. "There's no telling what could happen to you if I returned you to your home…or anywhere, for that matter. You're in danger."

I shake my head, thinking over everything that has happened over the past two weeks. How do I even know Lucien is telling the truth about all of this? What if he's lying to keep me here? It's not like I even know him or what he's capable of. "You…you're lying," I rasp out. "I don't believe you."

Lucien's eyes narrow as he regards me. "Why would I lie to you? I have no reason to."

"You lied before," I tell him, my voice unsteady. "You told me you'd let me go."

His hand clenches into a fist on the table. "I already explained to you why I can't let you go," he admonishes me.

"My father…and my fiancé…they would protect me!" I insist.

His brows furrow at my words, and he mumbles something under his breath that I can't hear. Then he says, "I don't think your fiancé will mind if I keep you a little while longer."

"What's that supposed to mean?" I ask, incensed.

Lucien glances up at me with a cocksure and shrewd expression on his face. "He's not even looking for you," he says with an unapologetic shrug.

I shake my head. "I don't believe you." We were mugged that night. Giovanni most certainly would have reported everything to the police, including the fact that I was kidnapped. And my father…my father would be looking for me. My father is a powerful man, maybe even more powerful than Lucien.

Tears fill my eyes as I glare at my remorseless captor. "You promised you would let me go after I gave you what you wanted." I choke back a sob. "You said…you said you let the others go. Was that a lie?"

"No. I let them go," he tells me.

"Then why won't you let me go? Why are you forcing me to stay here with you?" I cry. My words seem to visibly wound him, but I don't stop. "What do you want from me?" I shout. Standing up, I pound my fist on the table, rattling the surrounding dishes, and demand, "Tell me what you want from me!"

"More!" he snaps.

That single word makes me crumble as the truth finally comes out. He's not worried about my safety as much as he is about fucking me again.

My gaze meets Jackson's stare from across the table, and he looks worried. He gives me a subtle shake of his head, and I know he wants me to sit down and stop pushing his cousin.

Well, I'm tired of being a docile, little doll that everyone thinks they can just throw around and treat however they want.

"I don't want to stay here with you another second," I tell Lucien through gritted teeth. "I want you to let me go!" I scream, grabbing the first thing I see, which is my dinner plate, and throwing it. Pieces of fine china shatter and food splatters against the wall and floor.

Lucien stares at the mess with wide eyes. I can see the tremble start in his hands and work its way up his arms and entire spine. He stands and growls in frustration, shoving his large hands through his hair and pulling hard at the ends, threatening to rip each strand out by the roots.

He turns to me with a murderous glint in his eyes, and the look he gives me sends a chill straight through me to my very bones.

Jackson stands then, a worried expression etched on his face. "Luc," he says calmly, but Lucien doesn't even acknowledge his presence.

Lucien's gaze is pinpointed on me, and I know all he sees is red in that very moment. I watch in horror as he makes quick work of his belt buckle before pulling the leather through the loops. He bends the belt in half and slides it into his hands, squeezing it hard.

In one swift motion, he has me pinned against the table on my stomach and the skirt of my dress lifted up to my shoulders. The first blow is unexpected, and I cry out in shock from the pain. He hit me square on my bottom; the lacy material of my panties doing nothing to lessen the hurt.

The next few strikes are littered over my thighs and backside, but I bite my lip to keep from crying out again.

I won't give him the goddamn satisfaction.

My father has beaten me enough times in my life that I can tune the pain out. It will hurt later when the adrenaline wears off, but right now…I'm numb. He can hit me all he wants; it won't change a damn thing. I still want to go home, and I still…hate him.

Angry tears form in my eyes as he continues to beat me, but I refuse to let them fall. I refuse to give in. Not to him.

Lash after lash reins down on me, and I stay completely still, taking every bite of the leather across my sensitive flesh without so much as a flinch. This only seems to enrage him more, unfortunately.

Finally, I feel his hands leave my body as Jackson fights to pull him away. "Enough!" Jackson's loud voice echoes through the room. "Do you want to be like *them*?" he screams.

Immediately, the belt drops from Lucien's hand, clattering to the floor. I can hear him mumbling through his harsh, urgent pants. Gently, he pulls my skirt down to hide what he did. His rapid exhales whisper across my neck, but I don't dare move.

If there's one thing I learned growing up with an abusive father, it's that it's better to simply play dead. Just like in the animal world, it makes your attacker give up quicker if they think you're weak or too injured to fight back.

Spinning me around to face him, I see a pained expression on Lucien's face with perhaps…remorse laced into his features.

I don't even give him a chance to apologize for what he did. It's unforgivable. "You're a monster," I hiss at him, my voice trembling only slightly. My words seem to cut straight through him as he quickly releases his hold and takes a step back from me.

It's at that moment that Maria rushes into the room and surveys the mess on the floor. "Master Lucien," she says, out of breath. "I will clean it. Just give me a moment to ---."

"No!" he roars, and I jump at the sound of his deep voice echoing through the room. His hair falls rebelliously over his eyes as he points at me and says, "Number Seven made the mess, and she will clean it up."

Before I can even process the fact that he's resorted to calling me by my *number* and not my name, I watch Maria disappear into the kitchen, only to reappear a few seconds later with a caddy full of cleaning supplies.

Maria, the always strong, always confident, never taking anyone's shit kind of woman, is trembling in fright when she pushes the caddy into my arms, not even meeting my eyes. "Clean. Clean," she whispers, pleading with me and probably having no idea of the beating I just endured.

I glance at Jackson, who stands only a few feet away. He stays silent, but I can see the hard, disapproving stare he's giving his cousin.

The only eyes on me are from the one person I don't want to be staring at me. And if looks could kill, I'd drop dead on the spot. Lucien's cold glare sends a shiver up my spine. It's as if he's looking right through me.

Huffing, I set the caddy down and snap on a pair of sterile gloves. Then I retrieve a small, plastic garbage bag and begin to pick up the broken pieces of my plate and the larger pieces of food, placing everything into the bag.

"Start scrubbing the floor after you're done cleaning up your fucking mess. I want this entire room spotless," Lucien demands with a tight voice. Then he looks up at the others in the room and says, "Don't let her leave until it is."

And with that, he turns and leaves the room, leaving the three of us staring after him in bewilderment.

The entire room? That will take me all night. This room is bigger than most people's apartments.

Maria eventually brings me a bucket of water and adds a copious amount of some kind of anti-bacterial floor cleaner.

"I'll help," she whispers, but I wave her off.

"I made the mess. I'll clean it," I tell her before hiking my skirt up to my knees and kneeling on the floor. No one else should have to clean up after something I did. It was my decision to act out, so now I have to deal with the consequences...even if I'm already *feeling* them.

I grab a sponge, soak it in the soapy water and begin to scrub. My teeth sink into my bottom lip as I hold back my anger and my tears.

Angrily, I dump the sponge back into the soapy water and scrub the floor vigorously.

Jackson looms over me, and I can tell that he wants to say something. But he keeps his mouth shut, and so does Maria. No one needs to say anything that hasn't already been said. And besides, I'm too mortified to even talk to them right now.

I keep my face placid, schooling my features even though my knees are already starting to hurt from being pressed against the hard, unforgiving tile.

I scrub and scrub and scrub the floor even though it feels like knives are stabbing through my kneecaps, my back is so sore that it takes everything in me not to scream out in pain, my fingers are completely numb, and my entire backside and thighs feel like they're on fire from the beating I received earlier at the hands of that monster.

My body is screaming in protest, but I don't stop. I focus on the task at hand, wanting to complete it just to spite him. I'm sure Lucien expects me to break.

Well, he has another thing coming.

Because I won't break. Not now. Not ever. This is a cakewalk compared to what I've been through in the past. He just doesn't know that.

When I've gone around the entire room and am at the same place in which I had started, Jackson softly says, "That's enough, Adeline."

I stare down at my trembling hands that are red, sore and pruned from the water, and I begin to sob uncontrollably.

Everyone has their breaking point, and I guess I just reached mine.

Jackson's strong hands grip my arms. "Can you stand?" he whispers.

I shake my head. Gently, so gently, he helps me up, and I cry out as the pain I've been pushing out of my mind for hours assaults me all at once.

Jackson then scoops me up in his arms; and I collapse in exhaustion against his chest, breathing in his clean, masculine scent. "You are one tough chick," he tells me with a sad chuckle. Then he looks to Maria and says, "Bring my bag and a glass of water to my room."

To his room?

I stay quiet as Jackson carries me upstairs. He's strong, not even breaking a sweat when we reach the top of the tall staircase.

We go to the left, and my eyes widen when we pass by that god-awful bedroom I've been forced to stay in. To my relief, we continue down the hall, and he stops in front of a different door and pushes it open.

The room is large with several pieces of matching dark wood furniture, floor-to-ceiling windows and an en suite. A large, four-poster, king-sized bed rests in the center of the room on a geometric brown and blue rug with a fireplace nestled against the opposite wall. There are some clothes strewn about on the floor and a couple empty bottles of water sitting on the dark cherry writing desk. Jackson is clearly the exact opposite of his cousin. I can't imagine that Lucien lets a single piece of dirty clothing on the floor of his own bedroom.

Scowling and internally chiding myself for even thinking about my captor, I let out a soft sigh when Jackson lays me down in the middle of his bed on my stomach. The comforter is slightly rumpled, but the bed feels like heaven against my aching body.

I look up Jackson, and he gives me a small smile. "I'm sorry about what happened down there," he says softly. "Lucien can be…well, he's…" He stops talking and shakes his head, clearly wanting to apologize for his cousin, but not knowing where to start.

A soft pounding sounds on the door, and I jump. My hands fist into the sheets as I begin to shake, knowing who will be on the other side. Lucien's come for me. He's going to drag me back to that room and lock me in…or worse. And I don't know if I can survive worse right now.

"P-please," I plead to Jackson with wide eyes. I want him to hide me…or protect me, if that's even possible.

Jackson studies my reaction and frowns. "Relax. I'm sure it's just Maria."

I note that he has no fear of Lucien. I wish I could share his calm state, but I'm not able to relax until I see Maria standing on the other side of the door.

She hands Jackson a black, leather medical bag and a glass of water before quickly leaving as quickly as she came.

Jackson sets everything on top of his writing desk. Then, he opens up the split handles of the bag and roots around inside until he finds what he's looking for --- two bottles of pills. I watch him as he dispenses two pills into his palm before crossing the room.

Sitting on the edge of the bed, he holds the glass and pills out to me. "Muscle relaxer and pain pill," he explains. "They'll both make you pretty sleepy, but I'm sure you could use the rest," he says with a forlorn look.

I stare at the two white pills in his palm and frown. "Jackson, are you ---"

"Jax."

"What?"

"You can call me Jax. Jackson sounds so formal, don't you think?"

"Are you a doctor, Jax?" I ask, looking up at him.

"Yes," he answers. "Well, technically," he quickly adds. He watches me for a moment. "I can bring the bottles over if you want to read them, but I promise these won't hurt you." Then he adds, "I won't hurt you either."

I've had enough broken promises to last me a lifetime, but I decide to take Jackson at his word. Besides, the pain is becoming almost too much to bear. Snatching the pills and grabbing the glass from his hands, I down the pills with the water in a few quick swallows.

"Attagirl," Jackson says with a kind smile. He stands and strips out of his suit jacket, throwing it on the floor to add to the collection of dirty clothes in the corner of his room, and it almost makes me giggle how unlike Lucien he truly is. Then, he grabs the chair from his desk, spinning it around so the back is facing me before he sits down. "So, let's have a chat before you drift off into opioid dreamland." He sits and ponders for a moment before asking, "So what did you enjoy doing, you know, before you came here?"

I think about his question, but two things come to mind straightaway. "Well, I love books." I had a huge library at home filled with almost every book imaginable, and it was my safe haven. Most nights I would fall asleep with a book in my hand. "I also enjoy playing the piano."

His eyes light up. "Books and piano. Got it," he says as if he's storing the info away for later.

I study Jackson's handsome features and the stubble lining his strong jaw. He seems calm and…normal. His relaxed demeanor puts me at ease, but I still don't feel totally trusting of him. Mostly because he's Lucien's cousin. "When you said you're technically a doctor, what did you mean?" I ask.

"I didn't get my degree," he replies. "I quit halfway through my residency." He hangs his head sadly. "My father was sick…and it was impossible to concentrate on anything else but the cancer eating away at him. So, I made a choice," he says with a sigh. "I took care of him until he passed."

I can hear the emotion in his voice, and it makes me feel sad for him. "I'm sorry," I whisper.

His gray eyes slowly rise to meet mine. "Thank you," he says sincerely. "Anyway, I was top of my class, and I know more than most licensed practitioners." Then he adds, "I also majored in psychology while I was a pre-med student." Shifting his gaze to me, he says, "I mainly took the courses so that I could better understand Luc."

My brows furrow in confusion. I don't know much about my captor, but I know he has...issues, and that's putting it mildly. "What's wrong with him?" I blurt out.

"That's a good question," Jax says quietly. He closes his eyes and lets out a heavy sigh. "Lucien had a rough and terrible childhood. My dad found Luc and took him in when he was only a boy. We're the same age, but our relationship was bumpy, to say the least, those first few years."

"You didn't get along?" I ask, suddenly wanting to know more about Lucien's past.

"I wish that was as simple as that, but no, it was much, much worse. He was incredibly withdrawn and fearful of everything...and everyone." Jax folds his arms over the back of the chair and rests his chin on top of them. "It took some time, but my dad was eventually able to draw him out of his shell." He pauses. "If you only knew half of what I know..." His voice trails off, and I desperately want to know what he was going to say.

"What happened to him as a child?" I urge.

"I'm afraid that's his story to tell, not mine. I wouldn't betray Luc like that." He hesitates for a moment before adding, "I'll just say that if you knew what he'd been through as a boy, you would feel differently about him. You would understand why he is the way he is." He sits back in the chair. "He needs control and structure because he never had that as a child. He gained a lot of phobias and idiosyncrasies along the way even through his recovery, if you can call it that, but they are all justified, I assure you."

"How did he get the scars on his back? I felt them when we were, you know..." I can't even finish that sentence without feeling a hot blush running up my chest and neck.

"You...he let you *touch* him?" Jackson asks with a shocked expression on his handsome face.

"Yeah." My eyes drift close, but I force them back open. The pills he gave me must be kicking in. I'm certainly not as in as much pain as I was before. But I'm not ready to stop talking to Jax. I want to find out more about Lucien even if I hate him right now. For some reason, I have some sick need to understand him.

"I know he doesn't like being touched. Is that because of what happened to him as a kid? Did someone hurt him?"

Jax doesn't divulge any more than a simple nod.

"When Lucien was…hitting me, you had asked him 'Do you want to be like them'. What does that mean?"

"I was trying to get through to him by reminding him of what happened in his past. He was hurt by a lot of people, and I've never seen him lash out that way before. Quite frankly, it scared the shit out of me," he says with a shake of his head. "Lucien is so different with you, unpredictable, so unlike himself. You bring out this completely different side of him. It's amazing and terrifying all at the same time." He holds my gaze as he tells me, "I'm sure right now Luc is completely losing his mind in worry and regret over what he did to you, Adeline. If he could tell you he was sorry, I know that he would."

I can tell that Jax is very protective of his cousin, who is obviously more like a brother to him. I completely respect that. Lord knows my sisters never stuck up for me…even when I told them about our father beating me.

They all suffered the wrath of my father at some point in their lives, but I always got the brunt of his anger. He never locked any of them up and forbade them to have friends or even have a normal life, however. No. He saved all of his torment and rage for little old me.

"Where did you go just now?" Jax asks, his voice breaking me out of my thoughts.

I stare down at the comforter and pick at an imaginary thread. "I…I know what it's like to have a bad childhood. I'm sure I didn't suffer as much as Luc has." His nickname comes out so easily, but it feels strange on my tongue. I swallow hard past the lump forming in my throat before I continue. "My father…is not a good man. He used to hit me. A lot."

Jax moves closer, sitting on the edge of the bed by me, and I let him. "Go on," he prompts.

"I always had to be perfect for him. I was supposed to be a boy, you know, an heir to his empire, and I think he takes his anger out on me because I'm not." My eyes drift close again, but I force them open. "My mom died right after I was born, so he didn't have a chance for any more heirs. I'm it." My lower lip trembles. "He arranged a marriage between me and Giovanni, my fiancé. He wants me to give him the heir he never had with my mother."

The thought of my son being raised in the Italian mafia and running the Valenti empire someday suddenly seems like a travesty, and I don't know why I ever agreed to let my father marry me off in the hopes of giving him an heir.

I was so blind to everything before I came here. And if one good thing comes out of this whole thing, it's the fact that I'm wanting more for myself than simply being my father's little puppet. If I ever go home, things will never be the same. I won't allow them to be.

Placing a gentle hand over mine, Jax asks, "Do you love the man your father wants you to marry?"

"I think I was starting to fall for him, yeah. I think maybe we could have been happy one day." I worry my lip between my teeth. "But now…I don't even know what I want."

Jax pats my hand gently before withdrawing his. "You have plenty of time to decide. But trust me when I say, don't let anyone else control your fate, or you'll end up miserable."

I nod at his words of advice. "Thanks, Jax," I tell him, sleepily.

"I'm gonna go downstairs to mooch some food from Maria since our dinner was…well, you know. Sleep well, Addy. You're safe here."

My eyes are half closed while I watch Jackson leave his room and close the door. And then I start to drift off after that.

My dreams are plagued with the unknown…of how long Lucien will keep me here…and what he's going to do with me.

CHAPTER 23

LUCIEN

"YOU'RE A MONSTER."

What I did last night to Adeline…beating her with that belt…makes me exactly that --- *a fucking monster.*

I know what it feels like to be at the mercy of someone who is hellbent on hurting you. So, what the fuck would possess me to do that to Adeline?

The look on her face and the words she spit at me after it happened will be seared into my memory forever. If Jackson hadn't been there to stop me…who knows what would have happened. Would I have been able to stop on my own?

I don't know the answer to that question, and it fucking terrifies me.

I spent the better part of the night holed up in the gym, pounding away at the punching bag until my knuckles were sore and bruised, and then running full speed on the treadmill until I almost collapsed. After my punishing exercise routine, I huddled in the corner of my shower long after the hot water ran out. Shivering and freezing cold, I finally emerged from the safety of the glass-enclosed cocoon and managed to dress myself on autopilot.

I'm supposed to be working today, but I can't concentrate on anything but *her*.

Adeline is like the perfect distraction, the perfect drug, and I just want to keep injecting her into my veins like some sort of miracle cure.

I don't worry and obsess about everyone and everything when I'm around her. I'm so focused on her that there's no room for anything else in my troubled mind.

Is that why I'm refusing to let her go?

Keeping her here against her will makes me exactly what she called me --- a monster.

I told her I'm keeping her here because she's in danger, and she absolutely could be if her fiancé decides to sell her again. I highly doubt he'll get the opportunity to do that under Salvatore's nose again, but there is a small chance that he could.

And I'm not willing to take that chance.

The only solution I can come up with is keeping Adeline here on this island with me. I know it's selfish and wrong, but I don't care. I want her.

I need her.

Determined to get back to work, I turn my attention back to my computer, but find myself quickly accessing the camera feeds instead. I bring up Adeline's room, but find it…empty.

Panicked, I search the entire room and bathroom for any movement. Nothing. She's not in there.

"Where is she?" I growl in frustration.

Bringing up the feed from dinner last night, I watch in horror as I bend Adeline over the table and beat her with my belt. I force myself to watch, to take responsibility for what I've done, and it guts me.

I notice that the first strike made her jump and scream, but that she didn't make a move or sound with the strikes that came thereafter. I zoom in closer, and the expression on her face is a familiar one. She's blocking the pain out. And there's only one way she has mastered that.

She's been hurt before.

Scowling, I fast forward until the moment she's done scrubbing the floor. Her knees buckle as Jax scoops her up in his arms. I grimace. Not only did I beat her, but I made her scrub the entire fucking dining hall on her hands and knees.

I am a fucking monster.

I watch with intense curiosity as Jax carries Adeline to his room. She must still be there. With him.

Growling, I stand and make my way to Jax's room. I've never been jealous of my cousin before, but there's a first time for everything, I suppose.

I pound my fist on Jackson's door. When he opens it a minute later, he has a frown on his face. He's clearly disappointed with me, and it makes me feel a thousand times worse.

Raising my chin, I get a glimpse of Adeline sleeping on his bed. The rumpled sheets coupled with the fact that Jax is only wearing a pair of pajama bottoms fucking enrages me. My hands curl into fists at my sides as anger ripples through every muscle in my body. "Did you fuck her?" I hiss.

Jax pushes me out in the hallway and closes the door behind him. "Keep it down. She's still sleeping."

I stare at him in disbelief. "Well, did you?" I demand.

"No, of course not!" His words manage to slightly calm my internal rage, but now Jax is the angry one. "What the fuck happened last night, Luc?" he snaps.

"I fucking lost it," I growl. "Okay? I fucking lost it, Jax."

Some of his anger seems to dispel at my admission. "You're damn right you did. Adeline was terrified of you last night." He folds his arms across his chest. "So was I. Hell, we all were."

I mimic his posture, and we stand in the hallway with a thick tension hanging between us. I don't need a lecture from Jax. He already knows how fucked up I am. Why he remains here on this island with me, I have no idea. Sure, he leaves every once in a while for his own excursions and exotic desires, but he always returns.

He's like a loyal fucking dog that I don't always want shadowing me, but am thankful to have around anyway.

"How is she feeling?" I ask.

"She's been resting. I gave her some meds," he tells me.

"How bad is it? Her back isn't..." I struggle with my words. "I didn't scar her, did I?" Jax knows I got my scars from a particularly bad beating from my mother when I was nine years old. The metal buckle slashed through my delicate skin over and over again, leaving behind numerous open wounds that eventually healed on their own into rough and jagged scars.

The memory is as fresh in my mind as if it happened yesterday --- lying in the dark, damp closet she locked me in for days afterwards with no food, no water; my emaciated body covered in blood and shivering so hard my teeth chattered.

Sometimes, in my nightmares, I can still hear my own screams.

"You didn't hit hard enough to scar," he says, snapping me out of my reverie, and I breathe out a sigh of relief. "But she does have some pretty bad bruises."

I expected that. I'm just relived that her beautiful, flawless skin didn't get ravaged by my fucking psychotic episode. I truly don't think I would have been able to live with myself knowing that I scarred her.

"We talked a little last night," Jax says. "She's curious about you. Wants to know why you're...you," he says with a dark chuckle, but I don't find any humor in it. "I told her that it's your story to tell, Luc."

I nod. That's good that he didn't confide in Adeline. I don't need her fucking pity. Just like I don't need Jax's.

"Her father is the one who was beating her, not the fiancé."

"I see," I whisper.

"And it turns out she's in an arranged marriage of sorts. Salvatore is forcing her to marry Giovanni, but I think Adeline actually thinks she could fall in love with the guy, given the circumstances."

Grinding my teeth together, I try to process this new information. No wonder Giovanni had no qualms about selling her. If Salvatore is forcing him into the marriage, he probably doesn't even *like* the girl, let alone love her.

But Adeline thinks she could fall for him…or has she already fallen?

"How long are you keeping her here, Luc? You can't keep her forever. You know that, don't you?"

I glare at my cousin. "I'm not letting her go." Then I quickly add, "Right now."

His eyes narrow. "All right. I just hope you know what you're doing."

I hate the fact that he's questioning me, but I really hate the fact that I feel like I don't know what the hell I'm doing…about anything anymore, and especially not when it comes to Adeline. "I want her back in her room. *Today*," I demand.

He gives me a single nod.

I turn on my heel and leave, fuming at the fact that I left Adeline in Jax's room. I don't know why the thought of them together infuriated me so much, but I know deep down my fucked-up brain has already laid claim to her.

She's mine.

And I don't want Jax or anyone else to have her.

This obsession over her is driving me mad. I need to stay the fuck away from her for a while. I can't allow myself to have these *feelings*. It's such a foreign concept that it makes me angry to even think about someone, *this girl*, changing me.

She's under my skin in a way I never knew possible, and the darkness in me is slowly beginning to crack.

But I refuse to let any light into my black soul…even if it makes me a monster and even if it makes her hate me.

CHAPTER 24

ADELINE

IT'S BEEN FIVE days since I last saw Lucien, Jackson or had any human contact besides someone slipping in my meals three times a day.

The monotonous routine is messing with my head.

Wake up, shower, eat, nap, eat, pace, eat, go to sleep. Rinse and repeat. Rinse and repeat. Over and over and over again.

Without TV or so much as a magazine or book, I'm going stir-crazy, and I know this is all part of my punishment. Part of *his* plan.

And the thing is…it's working. I would do almost anything to go back to the way things were before I threw that dinner plate.

I don't know if it's cabin fever, a bout of deep depression, sheer loneliness, Stockholm syndrome or, hell, maybe all of the above, but I…*miss him*.

But above all else, *I need him.*

He is my only way out of this tedious regimen he's stuck me in. And at this point, I'm willing to do whatever it takes to get him to like me again and to stop punishing me for what I did.

And so when he enters my room on the fifth night, I can't contain that sick, deviant need from seeping out of every one of my pores.

I hear the tell-tale beeping sound before the knob turns. Knowing it's definitely not meal time since dinner was served a while ago, my gaze snaps to the door. I watch as Lucien calmly walks in. He's in a three-piece tailored suit, of course, but he looks…alarmingly strange.

I note that the top few buttons of his white shirt are open, revealing some of his muscular chest, and his tie is pulled loose from around his neck. His typically clean-shaven jaw is littered with day-old stubble, and his hair is mussed as if he just got done running his hands through it. All of these things are very uncharacteristic for him. Normally, he's perfectly put together. I've never seen him any other way.

And the sudden change in his demeanor has my spine going ramrod straight.

Did something happen? Is he going to let me go? Is he going to…hurt me again?

The bruises on my backside are finally fading, and I don't want to add anymore to the brutal collection.

I'm not sure of the cause of his distress. It's most likely me, but I don't know what other endeavors he has outside of this house. To be able to afford an entire staffed island, I would imagine he has his fingers in a lot of pies…and probably has a lot of illegal undertakings.

He calmly closes the door and leans up against the wall. His gaze is focused on the floor, and I almost want to scream at him to look at me. I'm so desperate for conversation, not having spoken to anyone in five whole days. I'm starting to forget the sound of my own voice.

Nervously, I chew on my bottom lip as I wait for him to speak. Minutes tick by, and the only sounds in the quiet room are my quick, panting breaths and his steady, sure ones.

Lucien looks like he is mulling something over in his mind. He opens his mouth to speak, but then snaps it shut without uttering a word and shakes his head absently.

"I---I'm sorry," I tell him, the words bursting out of my mouth when I'm not being able to take another minute of mind-numbing silence.

His eyes snap up to meet mine, and they narrow as if searching for any sign of deception on my face. I don't think he was expecting me to be the one apologizing after what happened. Quite honestly, neither was I. After all, it's not like I hit *him* with a belt.

He clears his throat before asking, "Have you learned your lesson?"

I nod empathically. And when his eyes narrow even further, I answer out loud, "Yes." I want to be out of this godforsaken room so badly that I would agree to and do almost anything at this point.

"Good." He straightens and makes a motion for the door, but I cry out for him to stop before he can leave. His back stiffens as his hand hovers over the keypad.

"Please don't leave," I utter, desperation saturating my voice. "Please. Stay." I'm so damn close to begging at this point.

He turns to me once more, his right eyebrow cocked. "You want me to stay here with you?"

I nod.

"Why?" he asks harshly, clearly thinking I'm trying to trick him somehow.

"I...I just..." My voice trails off. My emotions are at war with each other as I try to figure out what the hell is going on. His handsome features soften the longer I stare at him, and he almost looks...remorseful. Is he sorry for what he did to me? Did he come here to apologize, but didn't get the chance since I did it first?

Jax had told me that if Lucien could tell me he was sorry that he would. Given his troubled past, maybe Lucien has trouble expressing himself and apologizing even when he's clearly in the wrong.

How could I fault him for something out of his control?

I stare at him now, trying to picture him as a lost, sad, little boy. And given his current haphazard and uncharacteristic appearance, it's not hard to do just that.

I want to forgive Lucien, because I need him. Even if I don't want to admit it, I do. And despite the fact that he is the one holding me captive, I can't help but remember our first time together and how that night changed me forever.

I feel a familiar pull in my core as I stare into Lucien's dark eyes and crawl off the bed. I study him intensely as I walk towards him. His dark hair falls rebelliously over two pools of chocolate that appear infinitely deep. He's so incredibly handsome that it hurts to look at him.

How can I hate someone so much, but at the same time crave their touch and just the mere presence of them?

I nibble my bottom lip and stare at the floor. I know what I have to do to keep him here with me. A part of me is screaming in agony for me not to take the next step, but another part of me knows what must be done…and is turned on by it.

He watches me with a guarded look as I approach, observing me curiously. When I reach him, I drop to my knees on the plush carpet. My trembling hands reach for his belt, but he grasps them, holding them back.

"No," he tells me adamantly with a sharp shake of his head.

The intensity in which he stares at me sends a shiver through me. I stare down at his large hands holding my tiny wrists, and I realize that he's touching me…and not freaking out.

When I meet his gaze, I know that he's realizing the exact same thing. "Adeline," he says gruffly.

Gently, he cups my cheek in his palm, his thumb brushing away a stray tear I didn't even know I'd shed. And when his thumb caresses my lips, my tongue automatically darts out to lick the salty taste from his skin.

His eyes widen at the gesture, and he drags the pad of his thumb over my tongue and across my teeth, inhaling sharply, his breath catching in his throat.

I can see the lust in his eyes. I know he wants me. But the question is…do I really want him?

Do I even have a choice at this point?

Before I can second-guess what I'm doing, I wrestle out of his grip and go for the belt again. This time he doesn't stop me. The leather whispers against the belt loops as I pull. And then I unzip and unbutton his suit pants.

Feeling braver by the second, my hands stop shaking long enough for me to pull the material down his legs along with his boxer briefs. His erection springs up next to my face, and I stare at it in awe, wondering how he even fit inside of me our first time together.

Lucien's ragged, uneven breaths fill the room, and I peer up at him. "Can I put my mouth on you?" I ask him in a breathy whisper while clasping my hands behind my back to show him that I won't touch him with anything but my mouth.

He stares at me, his eyes drifting close for a moment before opening once more and locking me in an intense gaze. "Yes," he answers shakily.

His cock is long and not even fully hard yet, the large, smooth head glistening at the tip. My tongue slowly flicks out of my mouth to lick the salty drop from him.

That's when the first groan of pleasure wrenches from his chest, and it only spurs me on. For some unknown reason, I want to please him. I want to make him mine. I'm sure I'll regret all of this later, but I push down all of those thoughts and quiet my mind. I need to stay in this moment.

I lick around the crown over and over again, getting it nice and wet. His upper back falls against the wall as he watches my every move with half-lidded, lust-filled eyes while quick pants escape his lungs through parted lips.

His dick hardens to pure steel when I wrap my lips around the head of his cock and take him deeper into my mouth. I've never done this before, and so I'm not even sure I'm making him feel good. He stays quiet, his expression stoic, and I start to regret my decision to do this. I'm in way over my head at this point, not knowing whether he even likes it or not. When I begin to pull away from all the self-doubt running through my head, he suddenly snatches my hair in his hand.

"What --- why did you stop?" he asks, his gentle tone at odds with his rough hold.

"I don't know if I'm...doing this right," I whisper.

His grip in my hair lessens, and he gently grasps my chin and lifts it as he forces my gaze to meet his. "You've never done this before?"

I shake my head, and I watch as his eyelids droop and his nostrils flare. My admission clearly turns him on. "I've never let a woman give me head before," he confesses.

For some sick reason that turns me on and makes me feel almost...powerful. Feeling suddenly more confident, I wrap my lips around him once more. His head falls back against the wall as he lets out a long, shuddering sigh.

He's enjoying this. He just doesn't want to. He's all about control, and I realize that he doesn't want to give me any power over him. That's why he's never let anyone do this before. Because right now, in this situation, I hold all of his pleasure in my hands.

When his eyes are on me once more, watching me, I lick him from root to tip. A shiver takes over his body, and I can't help but grin. I move my tongue down to his balls, licking and sucking them into my mouth. This time, he can't control the groans coming from deep within his chest.

"Oh, fuck, Adeline," he growls out, and a shiver of arousal runs through me and straight to my core.

Squeezing my thighs together as I seek some sort of relief, I lick my way to the head before sucking him into my mouth once again. His hands grip my hair on either side of my head as he thrusts into my mouth, going deeper and deeper until I'm gagging.

"Fuck," he hisses through gritted teeth. "What are you doing to me, Adeline?" he whispers the question hoarsely as he pumps harder and harder. He's staring at me with such intensity that it floods my panties, and I squeeze my thighs together even harder, moaning around his cock.

Tears fill my eyes as I stare up at him, but I don't try to pull back. I place my hands on his thighs for support, but I don't push him away. I want him to use me, as wrong as that might be.

He growls my name loudly as he comes down my throat, and I swallow every drop of his release. His muscular thighs shudder under my touch, and his chest rises and falls rapidly with gasping, jagged breaths.

I'm in awe at the sight before me. I just brought the most powerful man I've ever met to his knees with pleasure.

When his breathing finally calms down, he releases the grip on my hair and stares down at me. "Get on the bed," he orders.

My cocky façade slowly crumbles away as I stand and slowly back away from him. Even though I've just done *that* for him, my mind is racing with what's right and what's wrong. I feel like I'm in a different world, not knowing which way is up as my knees hit the back of the mattress and my back hits the cool sheets.

My body trembles as I watch him step out of his pants and boxer briefs and remove his expensive shoes and socks. He stalks over to me; and, without hesitation, rips my pants down my legs. He stares at the lacy blue thong, and his tongue darts out to lick his full bottom lip. Gently, his fingers hook into the lace material, and he pulls them down to rid me of them also.

Feeling exposed, I crush my thighs together, but he frowns in disapproval at me. "I want to see you, Adeline," he says seductively.

Slowly, I open my legs, spreading wide for him. My breathing increases as he lies down on the bed between my legs.

"Beautiful," he breathes. The moment his finger touches my slit, I jump in surprise. "Relax," he says with a light chuckle. His dark eyes snap to mine as he says, "I want to taste you, Adeline, but I've never…I don't know if I…" His voice trails off, and he suddenly looks shy and unsure.

"It's okay, Luc," I tell him, using his nickname for the first time. That seems to get his attention, and his eyes return to mine. "I'm new to all of this too."

With a subtle nod, he returns his attention to my pussy. I watch as his tongue darts out of his mouth, and he licks the length of my already soaking wet slit. My hands fist in the sheets at my sides. Oh, god. Just one single lick, and I feel like I'm jetting off to the moon.

He licks me again and again and again until I'm biting my lip to stifle my cries. A hard slap to my inner thigh makes me gasp and wrenches a cry from my throat.

"Don't hold back, Adeline. I want to hear you fucking scream," he demands with a growl.

His fingers gently part my lips, and he begins to lick my clit. It feels like electricity going through my body, and I can't help the low, loud groan that rips from my throat.

"Yes, that's it," he whispers against me.

He devours me like a man that's starving, and I shamelessly buck against his face, wanting more and more. He licks and bites and sucks until I'm a writhing mess under him. His big, strong hands grasp my thighs, holding me down and not allowing me to escape even an ounce of pleasure coming from his mouth, and all I can do is tremble and cry out as I enjoy the ride.

Lucien pushes a finger inside of me then, and I gasp at the intrusion. He works his thick finger inside of me for a few seconds before adding another finger, pumping them both in and out of me and bringing me to the precipice faster and faster.

Then, his fingers curl inside of me, and my back suddenly bows off the bed. Whatever he's doing to me, it's driving me crazy. The sensation is so overwhelming that I begin to try to pull away from him. "Please, no," I beg. "I can't."

With his free hand, he grips my thigh tightly so that I can't move away and continues his assault. "It's okay. It's okay, baby," he says soothingly.

I'm stunned by the term of endearment he used, and the line between unwilling captive and willing paramour blur drastically. Eventually, I stop fighting him and allow the pleasure to take over me.

His tongue assaults my swollen little button as his fingers work my inner walls, and it's too much. I fall over the edge of the cliff, crying out in pleasure as my body is wracked with a soul-obliterating orgasm. I can feel the wetness seeping from me, and he groans in approval. Wave after wave crashes over me, and I can't stop myself from crying out his name.

He growls possessively against my skin, consuming me as the torturous pleasure goes on and on until I'm completely wrung out. Exhausted, I collapse against the soft sheets, breathing heavily, my heart threatening to beat out of my chest.

He gives me one last lick, which causes a tremor to rock through my entire body. And then I feel all of his warmth leave me as he climbs off the bed.

I press my palm to my erratic heartbeat, feeling it begin to slow as I gradually come back to earth. The rustling of clothes grabs my attention, and I sit up to see him getting dressed. He has a guarded, stony look on his face just like after the first time we had sex, and it tears me apart.

It's déjà vu all over again when I see the same emotions written on his face --- loathing and regret.

Tears gather in my eyes as I quickly grab the sheet to cover myself. He was in the moment both times when we were succumbing to our desires. But as soon as the moment's over, it's as if a switch goes off inside of him and he becomes distant and detached.

I hate it. I hate how quickly he can dismiss me as if I'm nothing but a toy to be played with and then put away when he's done manipulating me.

Lucien gives me one last, long glance before he leaves.

Shocked, I sit there for a while replaying what just happened over and over again in my mind. He left without saying a word, making me feel like some kind of cheap whore. Thinking about myself down on my knees earlier…that's exactly what I was.

I was so deprived of attention and affection that I just whored myself out to the man who's keeping me captive without considering the consequences.

Feeling used and utterly broken inside, I sink under the expensive sheets and plush comforter and cry until I'm numb.

CHAPTER 25

LUCIEN

I LEAVE ADELINE'S room in a hurry and run right into a hard chest. *Jax.* The fucking voyeur was listening…once again. Hell, maybe he was even *watching*, for all I know.

"Fuck, Luc. I'm beginning to think you need to start giving me some pointers," he says with a shit-eating grin.

I glare at him, instantly regretting giving him the code to my office where I know he can access the camera feeds. His perversion of watching other people have sex is becoming a nuisance. I'm furious that he once again listened to Adeline crying out *my* name.

Mine.

He's already had Adeline in his bed. I know nothing happened between them, but I can't help but wonder if Adeline finds him attractive. What if she wants Jax more than me? Fuck, just the thought of it drives me insane. I don't want to share her in any way with anyone.

"Fuck you, Jackson," I hiss, seething, as I push past him and go straight to my room.

I slam the bathroom door shut and pace the floor with my hands clenched into fists at my sides and my brain running a mile a minute.

Scowling, I turn on the hot water and step under the spray. Usually my shower is a refuge, but right now I can't escape here or anywhere, for that matter. *That girl.* That girl has crawled under my skin and become a new obsession for me. My OCD has taken a backseat, and she has slithered her way to the forefront of my mind. I can't stop thinking about her. I can't stop wanting her. And even when I have her, it's not enough.

And my biggest fear is that I'll never be able to get enough of her.

I can't keep her. I know that. She has a life and a family to return to. When I think about her returning to that scumbag fiancé, though, my hackles rise and I want to punch someone in the fucking face. He *sold* her to me. I could have raped her and strangled her…even murdered her. He has no idea who I am, what I'm capable of. And yet, he allowed her to come to me without a care in the world.

What if I would have been someone else? I'm not saying I'm a saint, by any means, but I'm not a ruthless sadist. Would he have sold her to another? *Will* he sell her to another when she returns to him?

The thought of anyone else touching her drives me insane. I scrub my skin raw and growl out in frustration. I've put myself in a vulnerable situation where I feel like I've lost total control, and *I fucking hate it.*

I'm always in control. *Always.* And I haven't experienced this helpless feeling of loss of power in a long time. In my adulthood, I've always taken what I've wanted. I never took an unwilling woman, but I commanded her, possessed her, drove my cock into her relentlessly until she begged for more.

That experience with Adeline just minutes ago made me feel helpless…but also so damn good. Her mouth on my cock… Fuck, I'm getting hard again just thinking about it. She is so innocent and unsure of herself that it turns me the fuck on. I want to be her first for everything, and that scares the living shit out of me.

I've never wanted anyone as much as I want her.

After I finish my shower, I go through my usual routine a little more quickly and sloppier than usual. I have a desperate need to get to my office and check on Adeline. She's like a drug to me, and I need a fucking hit.

I dress in a simple long-sleeved shirt, boxer briefs and cotton pajama pants before leaving my room in a hurry. I force myself not to run to my office, but I get there in record time.

Needing to see her again, I bring my computer back to life and click on the camera monitors strategically placed in her room. The sight on the screen has me creasing my brows in confusion. I hit the volume key a few times to bring up the sound. And that's when I hear it.

Adeline is…crying.

Her body wracks with sobs under a mountain of bedding, and I can almost feel her heartache seeping into my bones. I slide my chair back and rest my elbows on my knees and my chin in my hands. I don't understand why she's so upset. The only thing I can think of that I might have done wrong is leaving without telling her goodbye. Or perhaps me leaving period is what I did wrong.

All this shit is new to me, and I couldn't possibly make her understand all of my hang-ups.

I've never slept beside a woman. I've never cared enough to stay for more than a few moments after. None of the other girls ever cared. They were more than happy to get their money and be on their merry way to their brighter and definitely more luxurious future.

But I told myself from the very beginning that Adeline isn't like all the others. She's different, a unique diamond in the rough.

I lift my gaze and watch her with rapt concern as she continues to cry, and I suddenly feel sick to my stomach. The notion that I could be worried about someone else's feelings is alarming, to say the least. I've been such a cold-hearted bastard for so long that I didn't think the black hole where my heart used to belong could ever begin to beat again…especially not for a woman, and most certainly not one that I *purchased*.

CHAPTER 26

LUCIEN

"MARIA SAID THAT Adeline's refusing to eat," Jax tells me over breakfast one morning.

The eggs I've been chewing suddenly taste like wet cement, and I take a big swig of freshly squeezed orange juice to wash the lump down my throat.

It's been a few days since I last went to Adeline's room. I had gone there to apologize for hitting her with my belt, an act so unspeakable considering my dark past; but instead, she surprised me by saying *she* was sorry before I could even get up the courage to do it.

Then, the unthinkable happened…she dropped to her knees and gave me the most amazing, and my first ever, blow job. I reciprocated the favor, licking her pussy until she gushed her sweet cream all over my face. Also a first for me.

I still can't believe what happened between us. It was like an out of body experience, pleasuring her in a way I've never done before and never thought I'd be capable of doing.

I've only ever wanted a woman once. After I've taken her virginity, she suddenly became spoiled and unwanted in my eyes. But not with Adeline. It's like I just fucking can't get enough of her.

When I'm with her, I feel...normal. I feel like I can be who I long to be, not who I've become.

But as soon as the moment we'd shared was over, I could feel the sick part of my brain taking over. Counting the seconds until I could get in the shower and wash her scent and fluids off of me. The nauseating feeling creeped up my spine until I almost gagged right in front of her.

The silence in my head that I feel when I'm around her is only short-lived. My brain only shuts off for a short period of time until it reboots itself, bringing all of my fears and obsessions back with a vengeance.

I have spent the better part of the past three days in the shower, ridding myself of her taste and her touch, rubbing my skin raw and bloody under scalding hot water.

But in all actuality, I didn't even want to get rid of her scent. I wanted to let it consume me.

If only I could control my thoughts and actions...if only I had a choice...

Jackson snaps his fingers in front of my face, snapping me back to reality. "Did you hear what I said? She's miserable and starving herself."

I give him a small nod. I know she's not been eating. And I know she cries almost every second of every day.

That's because I watch her. Constantly. I'm obsessed with everything about this girl.

I thought I could ignore her and my feelings towards her, but it feels like I'm going through withdrawal from the most powerful and purest drug in the world. Adeline is a cure for a lot of my neuroses, but I'm quickly coming to realize that there is no cure for *her*.

However, I can't seem to bring myself to go back to her room, to apologize and to make things right.

I know why she's upset. Because I'm a total fucking asshole. I took what I wanted from her…*twice*…and left her right after, probably making her feel less than a worthless whore.

"I need to apologize to her," I tell Jax. "But I…can't."

"You can't, or you don't know how?" he asks with a knowing smile.

He always was good at reading me. "I tried," I start, but then pause. "Things didn't…end so well between us last time."

He cocks his head to the side as he regards me. "It *sounded* like things ended well between you two," he says with a chuckle.

"Fucking voyeur," I mutter under my breath, gritting my teeth at his words. "I mean, I left her right after, and she was upset about that." I can only imagine the expression on my face as the wicked thoughts in my head were running rampant. She probably thinks I hate her or don't care about her at all.

But that couldn't be further from the truth…no matter how much I want to deny it and lie to myself.

"Well, locking her in a room twenty-four seven is probably driving the poor girl mad."

I shake my head at him. "I can't just…let her go." I don't even want to dwell on the overwhelming feeling in my chest when I think about her leaving this island…leaving me.

"Then give her something to do…maybe a little bit more freedom, something better than staring at four walls every day." Jax picks at the eggs on his plate and nonchalantly says, "She loves books."

My interest perks up. "She told you that?"

"Yeah," he murmurs around a mouthful of food.

I turn away from him, feeling repulsed. He knows that shit drives me crazy. Just the sound of his lips smacking together and the grinding of his teeth as he chews almost sends me into a tailspin.

Closing my eyes and pinching the bridge of my nose to ward off the dizziness, I ask him, "What kind of books? What are her favorite authors?

What kind of genres does she like?" The questions come tumbling out of my mouth in quick succession.

Jax thankfully swallows before he answers me. "She didn't say. She just told me she loves to read and play piano."

I think about the white baby grand sitting in the library. Currently, the shelves are only one-third stocked in the great two-story room. But I could order more.

I could order a hell of a lot more.

Suddenly, I push away from the table and walk out of the room.

"Where you goin'?" Jax calls after me.

"Starting on my apology," I respond before making my way to my office.

* * * * * * *

HOURS AFTER BREAKFAST with Jax, my fingers grip the pen tightly as I scrawl down every book I can think of. I've filled out almost a hundred post-it notes, and I force myself to stop. Moving my cramped hand to the mouse, I begin to click and order, click and order and click and order until I've spent thousands upon thousands of dollars on a shipment of solely books.

I realize I'm trying to appease Adeline, trying to make her comfortable here…even though she doesn't want to stay. A part of me likes to think that she would stay on her own; but I think given the opportunity, she would run at first chance.

And I won't let that happen.

I can't let her go back to a fiancé who would rather sell her than wed her. Back to her father, who would rather keep her under lock and key than give her an ounce of freedom. Back to a life that's infested with so much darkness that it will surely smother her light. Back to a world…without me to protect her.

Shaking my head, I finish up ordering, paying extra for expedited shipping and setting up all the details with my trusted man on the mainland who will fly the shipment in tomorrow morning.

And then I set to work on creating something that will allow Adeline more freedom…even if the thought of her being free scares the living shit out of me.

CHAPTER 27

ADELINE

I'VE ALWAYS TRIED to be a silver lining kind of girl, even when my life seemed rather dull and meaningless. Even when my father kept me locked away in an ivory tower, leaving me with only two options --- isolation and reading. I read to keep myself occupied, but I also read to escape. Books allowed me to leave my prison and venture into new worlds, discover new places and make new friends.

Being the youngest of seven girls, my father wanted to protect and shelter me from everything. When you live in a mafia world, someone is always trying to take what's yours. My sisters were easy targets, and they suffered profoundly for my father's life of crime and power.

I'd heard a lot of stories over the years. They keep me awake at night sometimes, thinking about how my sisters were tortured, body parts sent to my father piece by piece until there was nothing left.

Out of seven of us, only three remain living, including me. The four oldest had been kidnapped over the years, held for ransom or simply killed for retribution. My father never caved, never gave into the kidnapper's demands. Not even once.

He allowed them all to die horrible deaths, and he justified it by saying that he wouldn't appear weak to his enemies…even if it meant that all of us would have to die someday in the same manner our oldest sisters did.

And that's why I have given up hope of getting saved from this island. No one is coming for me. No one is going to save me. I have to leave on my own.

If Lucien thinks locking me in this room is going to break me, he's sadly mistaken. I've been locked up my entire life. So being kept in one room for an extended period of time is nothing new. I just wish I had a book or two to read to help me mentally escape from this monotonous hell. The complete and utter boredom is the only difference from this *new* prison and my *old* prison.

I'm simply…biding my time, waiting for the right opportunity to strike. And I have to believe that it will.

My empty stomach grumbles ferociously, and I grimace. I have been starving myself in the hopes that an opportunity will come quickly. If I understand my captor as well as I think I do, he won't let me starve.

The door opens, pulling me from my thoughts. Lucien steps into the room, looking handsome in his usual attire, a dark, tailored three-piece suit.

I stare at him, warily. It feels like all the air has just been sucked out of the room. He emits this dark and powerful presence that takes my breath away.

He must notice my uneasiness, because his brows furrow as he stares at me. "I…I want to show you something," he says softly, and I can almost hear something in his tone that sounds like excitement.

I'm not buying it. Just when I think I have Lucien figured out, he always surprises me. "W-what is it?" I stammer, feeling the unease creep into my bones.

"You'll like it," he says, flashing me a grin.

I think it's the first time I've ever seen him smile. The expression transforms his face to make him even more impossibly handsome.

I don't want to think of my captor as attractive, because I know what lies under that handsome exterior --- *a monster.*

He opens the door wider and steps out into the hall, looking back at me. "Come," he mutters.

Having no choice but to do as he says, I slowly stand and go to him.

I'm hesitant at first, cautiously stepping over the threshold, afraid of what awaits me on the other side. When I see nothing but an empty hallway, I blow out a soft sigh of relief. He hasn't let me out of my room since Jax made me return after that dramatic blowup I had at dinner when I realized he wasn't releasing me like he had promised.

We go to the end of the hall and down the steps. Then he takes me into a wing of the house I didn't even know existed. I feel my steps faltering as he leads me towards two giant hand-carved doors.

He stops and turns to me then, the rare smile prominent on his face once again. "What's in that room?" I ask, my voice tremulous.

"Nothing bad," he tells me after no doubt hearing the fear in my tone. And then he says, "I promise."

I narrow my eyes at him. The last time he promised me something, he went back on his word. So why the hell should I trust him now? My entire body is tense as I wait for him to open the doors, expecting the worst.

But when I slowly open my eyes and take in the room that lies before me, I gasp in surprise. "Oh!"

My feet are moving before my brain can even stop me, and I turn, doing a complete circle in the middle of a gigantic library. It's two stories tall with a staircase on the right of the room leading up to the top floor. There's a fireplace in the corner with a white baby grand piano situated in front of it. And books, gazillions of books, books about animals, fantasy books, sci-fi, romance, every book by every author, even some of my favorites, imaginable litter the beautiful, hand-carved wooden shelves.

Tears fill my eyes as I go to the long shelf to my left. My gaze skims the titles, and I instantly begin pulling out book after book, stacking them in my arms. I'm like a kid in a candy store right now, and I feel the sudden urge of happiness and belonging. Libraries have always been like sacred havens to me.

Lucien's chuckle behind me breaks my spell. I slowly put the stack of books down on a nearby table and turn to look at him. He looks happy as if I've made him happy somehow. But why?

"M-may I take some books back to my room?" I ask, crossing my fingers that he'll grant me this one small respite.

He stares at me for a long moment before he answers. "You may read in here, if you'd like. I'll come collect you later when it's time for you to go back to your room."

His words shock me, and I'm so caught off-guard by the generous offer that I can't help myself when I run to him and wrap my arms around him in a hug. "Thank you!" I exclaim against his chest.

I feel his body stiffen under my grip. And when I realize what I've just done, I quickly release my hold on him and take a few steps back. A blush creeps up along my neck and face as I mutter, "Sorry."

He clears his throat before mumbling, "Enjoy your time in here." And then he leaves, leaving me completely alone in this beautiful library.

I stare at the door long after he leaves. I don't know what came over me just a few moments ago. The solitary confinement has definitely done a number on me. I was so thankful for a few hours in the library that I…*hugged* my captor?

Shaking my head, I push my reaction to the library aside and go back to the stack of books I picked out. Lucien has given me a great gift, and I don't intend to waste a second of it.

But as I pick up the first book, all I can seem to think about is the grin on his face at making me happy and how good it made me feel to see him finally smile.

CHAPTER 28

LUCIEN

I EXPECT HER to run.

I study her for hours on the video feed. And to my shock and utter surprise, Adeline stays in the library, cuddled up on a leather chaise lounge with a navy blue throw…reading…and eating. I had Maria fix her some hot tea, a sandwich and some homemade cookies. Adeline practically devoured them in between turning pages, and I couldn't be happier that her hunger strike is clearly over.

Her love for books is obvious, but I honestly thought her need to escape would trump everything else.

Evidently, she's come to the conclusion that she's not leaving here. Not easily, at least. And the sooner she understands that and comes to terms with that fact, the sooner we can continue on with what we had started weeks ago.

I would give anything to feel her under me again, her body opening up to me like a beautiful flower and responding to my touch so fervently. Just being in the same room as her drives me insane. A part of me wants to force her down to the ground and just take what's rightfully mine that I bought and paid for. But another, much bigger part of me wants her willing and compliant. I just want her to want me the same way I want her.

However, I'm not an idiot. I know she will never like me that way. She will never see me for anything other than what I clearly am --- her captor.

The pad of my thumb skims across the screen over her pretty face, and I'd do almost anything right now to be able to touch her for real.

When I drop back in my chair and realize I don't have the compulsion to clean my thumbprint from the screen, I feel like a different person. I feel…almost normal.

Adeline makes me want to be a better person, someone who can make her happy. When I think back to the look on her face and her emerald orbs glistening with tears by just letting her *read*, the black, tarry muscle in my chest began to beat through the everlasting darkness again.

Sighing contentedly, I think back to what Jackson said to me. Adeline needs some sort of freedom, even if I'm not willing to let her go. He's completely right. I can't keep locking her up like some sort of Disney princess in my fucked-up fairytale.

Turning my attention back to the project I've been working on, I just need to make a few more final touches until it's ready.

And then Adeline will have some of the freedom that I know she's been craving.

* * * * * * *

IT'S LATE WHEN I finally call it a night. I check the camera feed in the library and see that Adeline is still resting comfortably and reading on the leather chaise.

Jax certainly wasn't kidding when he said she loves books. She's utterly infatuated with them, it appears.

My eyes are glued on her when I see her yawn and set down the book she just finished. She stands and walks towards the door.

My heart skips a beat, thinking this is it. This is when she tries to run.

But Adeline surprises me when she stops in front of the baby grand piano. Her eyes scan the length of the instrument as if admiring a beautiful and rare creature. Then, she pulls out the small bench and takes a seat.

I lean up in my chair, completely engrossed with the screen. I watch her delicate hands lift the fallboard, staring at the black and white keys with a serene look on her face.

Standing, I leave my office, my feet carrying me before my brain can even comprehend my next move. I have a sudden urge to hear her fingers gliding along the ivory keys. I don't care if she can't play anything other than *Chopsticks*. Just the idea of seeing and hearing her play sets my blood on fire.

I force myself not to burst through the door; and instead, slowly and gently open it, as to not startle her.

Adeline doesn't so much as blink when I enter. It's as if she's in some kind of trance...or maybe she knew I would be coming for her and was expecting me.

My feet stay planted several feet away, and I just silently watch her. Jackson told me she plays, so I don't even bother asking her. After a long pause, I finally request, "Will you play for me?"

Her brows furrow slightly as an unreadable expression slides over her face. I expect her to tell me no. But she surprises me by asking, "What would you like me to play?"

I shrug, not knowing the extent of her skills. "Whatever you'd like," I tell her.

She faces the piano and stares at the keys for a moment. When her delicate fingers line up on the keys and begin to play, I immediately recognize the music. It's Beethoven's Moonlight Sonata.

I'm completely mesmerized as I watch her play the somber music perfectly striking each key with precision. She's definitely a practiced pianist. That much is clear. She plays elegantly.

Her face looks so serious, and her brows are furrowed in concentration, but she doesn't mess up...not even once.

Once again, Adeline has amazed me beyond belief.

I swallow hard as I walk in a slow arc behind her. I'm completely enraptured as she plays, and this isn't the first time she's caught me in her seductive web. This woman has totally beguiled me in such a short time. It's almost as if she were made for me right out of my very own dream. Suddenly the cheesy line, where have you been all my life, comes to mind.

Her eyes are hooded, and it reminds me of when I took her for the first time, as if she's right on the edge of ecstasy.

I watch her skilled, delicate fingers fly over the keys, and I can feel my cock straining against my zipper. Fuck, I want her. And I'm starting to think I'll never be able to get enough of her.

"When did you start playing?" I ask softly, afraid of breaking her out of the trance she's in.

"When I was five," she whispers, and I can hear the sadness in her tone.

Five? Fuck, when I was five I was barely able to count to ten. My mother rarely sent me to school and never taught me how to do anything but steal and get her money to buy drugs.

Adeline and I obviously had very different upbringings. Even though hers would be considered glamorous to some, I have a feeling it wasn't. With a father like Salvatore Valenti, I don't see how it could have been. He's a ruthless, evil man, and I've heard the stories about how many of his daughters wound up in pieces on his doorstep. He has a reputation for being untouchable, and it only took his daughters dying for his enemies to realize how true that was.

"Do you enjoy playing?" I ask her.

"When I'm not forced to, yes," she answers solemnly.

I frown at her response. Does she mean when she was home, or does she feel like I'm forcing her now?

"My piano teacher always made me practice the same boring concertos over and over again until it felt like my fingers were going to bleed."

Okay. So maybe she doesn't mind playing for me then. I hope not, because, quite frankly, I could listen to her play forever. She's elegant and absolutely stunning as she sits perfectly on the edge of the bench, her fingers moving swiftly and her foot softly tapping the pedal below.

Not being able to stand it any longer, I reach out and touch her delicate neck. She flinches from my touch, having been so engrossed in the music that her hand slips off the keys, making a sour note.

She gasps and says, "I'm sorry," looking up at me with undiluted fear in her emerald eyes.

I frown, wondering why her messing up would cause such a reaction. The realization dawns on me slowly. Obviously perfection has been demanded of her for her entire life. She was locked away by her father, probably kept from the outside world.

And I'm doing the same exact things to her. The things she *hates*.

I step back from her, suddenly needing the space. I curl my fingers into a fist, the lingering touch of her skin seemingly burning its way into my flesh like a branding.

"I think it's time for you to go back to your room now," I tell her quietly, and secretly hating the way my voice comes out callous.

She gives me an almost imperceptible nod and stands from the piano, gently lowering the fallboard and pushing in the bench. I watch as she looks longingly back at the books, and I can almost hear the question in her mind.

"You can take some books to your room, if you'd like," I tell her. Her gaze snaps to mine, perhaps wondering if I somehow read her thoughts.

A slow smile appears on her face, making her impossibly more beautiful, and I can practically feel the happiness exuding from her every pore as she runs over to the nearest shelves and grabs several romance, thriller and mystery books, piling them high in her arms.

As I help her carry the books up to her room, Adeline chatters on about her favorite authors and how she got lost in one of their books today and lost complete track of time.

"I enjoy Tolkien myself," I tell her, naming one of her favorites. The ease in which we're carrying on a normal conversation does not escape me.

Adeline proceeds to tell me how much she loves *The Lord of the Rings* series. "Oh, and have you seen the movies?" When I shake my head, she continues by spiritedly saying, "They're not as good as the books, of course. Movies never are. But the director, Peter Jackson, did a great adaptation." She stops talking and takes a breath, chuckling lightly. "Sorry I'm rambling." She flashes me a shy smile. "It feels like forever since I just...talked with anyone."

I grimace inwardly at her words. It's my fault she feels that way. Before I can even stop myself, I suggest, "We could watch the movies sometime."

The myriad of emotions that play over Adeline's face over the next few seconds make my heart stutter. At first she's excited, but then obviously confused and then lastly forlorn. "Sure," she says quietly.

I open the door to her room, and she steps inside. She takes the books from me, and her fingertips graze against my forearms. My eyes flutter close. I'm awaiting the barrage of malevolent thoughts, but they don't come. All I can think about is...*her*.

When I open my eyes, Adeline is looking up at me with those emerald orbs that give me a glimpse into the beautiful soul that lies beneath.

"Thank you for the books, Lucien," she says, my name a caress on her lips and her tone no longer contains the revulsion I'm used to hearing.

"Goodnight, Adeline," I tell her.

"Goodnight," she whispers with a sweet smile.

I close the door, placing my palm against the wood as I hear the beep signaling that she's locked away for safekeeping.

And I know if I had it my way...Adeline would never leave.

I would keep her forever.

CHAPTER 29

ADELINE

SO MUCH HAS changed over the past week. Lucien has actually been...nice to me. I don't know why or how, but I've stopped questioning it. We've been eating our meals in the dining room together every evening, sometimes with Jax and sometimes just the two of us, and he's been giving me more time in the library where my mind just gobbles up book after book after book.

It's a welcome reprieve from reality, and I couldn't be happier about it. Although, if I'm being completely honest, my reality hasn't really been all that bad lately.

However, the more I'm around Lucien, the more confused I become, because I have a dark, looming cloud of doubt if my feelings are truly genuine or not. I don't know if I've completely lost my mind or if I have a bad case of Stockholm syndrome; but the more time I spend with Lucien, the more I've grown to like him. And when he's not around, I actually miss him. I know what I'm feeling sounds crazy, but I can't help it.

I'm growing to *like* him.

He's smart and handsome, and his smile, although rare, could melt even the coldest of hearts.

It's late in the afternoon, and I'm curled up, reading in bed when Lucien unexpectedly comes to my room. Usually I don't see him until around dinnertime, and so I'm surprised…and *happy* for his visit.

"Hello, Adeline," he says when he enters, and I can't help but love the sound of my name coming out of his mouth. He's wearing a grin that has become a constant accessory as of late. It's nice to see him smile so much.

"Hi."

I notice that he's carrying a small, white box in his hands, and my interest is instantly piqued. He catches my gaze and stares down at the box. "I have a present for you," he tells me. "Well, two actually," he adds quickly.

He closes the distance between us in a few long strides and hands the box to me. I take it from him without any hesitation, and it surprises me. We've definitely developed a level of trust between the two of us recently, against all odds.

I carefully lift the lid and smile when I see the contents. Inside is a digital watch with a rose gold wristband. Since there are no clocks in my room, I've been going insane from never knowing what time it is.

"It's perfect," I tell Lucien with a big smile.

"I'm glad you like," he says. And then he flashes that drop-dead gorgeous smile of his that seems to always make my heart go pitter-patter.

I take the watch out of the box, setting the contents down and wrapping the band around my wrist. Struggling with the clasp on the band, I gasp when Lucien gently takes my wrist in his hands and does the clasp for me.

His fingers are long and adept, and I close my eyes, remembering the feel of his hands on me. He's only a few inches away from me now, and I wonder if he can hear my heart beating out of my chest.

"I have one rule about this, Adeline." When I meet his gaze, he says, "*Never* take this off. It's waterproof, so you don't have to worry about even taking it off when you shower."

I nod in agreement to his demand, and I can't help but wonder if there's something sinister about this watch like it has a tracker to monitor my movements or something. But then I decide I don't care. It's not like he doesn't know where I am twenty-four-seven already. I'm sure there are cameras everywhere throughout and outside of the mansion at his control. And it's not like I can just up and leave an *island* anyway without his knowledge.

"You won't need to charge it. I installed some new thermoelectric technology I've been working on. The watch will stay charged running solely on your body heat."

It takes a moment for his words to register. "You…you *made* this?"

He nods. "I bought some of the pieces that I couldn't make on my own. Mostly, I did all the internal work, writing the software for the hardware and installing the thermoelectric modules."

"Wow, Lucien," I say while peering down at the watch that seems so much more than just a watch to me now. I've known from the start that Lucien was intelligent, but I didn't know he was a borderline genius. My eyes flash to his as I tell him, "That's incredible."

Lucien gives a small shrug as if it's nothing, and I have a feeling he's not used to getting compliments.

"What's the other present?" I ask, remembering that he told me he had two gifts for me.

He turns and walks over to the keypad by the door. I frown when I think he's about to leave without telling me, but then watch in confusion when he begins to type a long code into the keypad. I hear three beeps before a *click* on the door latch, and the keypad goes dark.

"I'm allowing you to leave your room whenever you'd like. You may come and go as you please."

My mouth falls open at his words.

"But make no mistake, you're not allowed to leave this house. I have guards present outside at all times, and they are aware of your…boundaries," he says carefully.

I can't help but be a little displeased by his demand. I would love to feel the sun on my face and the breeze in my hair. It's almost springtime, and I always loved to watch butterflies and plant flowers when I lived with my father. "Will I ever be allowed outside?" I boldly ask.

"Yes, when a certain level of trust is earned," he answers honestly.

I can't help but be excited about the prospect of being able to go outside. "Thank you," I tell him. "For everything."

He gives me a small smile. "You're welcome, Adeline."

My name rolling off of his tongue sends a shiver up my spine, and I involuntarily take a few steps towards him. When I realize what I'm doing, I stop short and shift my gaze to meet his dark eyes. What was I about to do? Touch him? Kiss him?

Oh, god, I'm losing it, I tell myself.

Lucien stares at me for a beat before he says, "See you at dinner."

The door closes behind him, and it seems odd not hearing the beeping noise and the lock engaging. This newfound sense of freedom has me almost giddy even though I know it's wrong to feel that way.

I shouldn't be happy about being allowed to leave a room I've been locked up for only god knows how long.

But I am.

I am happy.

It's so hard to differentiate between right and wrong anymore that I try not to dwell on it. Normal rules don't apply here, and I'm not the person I used to be.

And as long as I'm here, I might as well get used to the new way...even if I'm afraid of losing myself in return.

CHAPTER 30

LUCIEN

THE WATCH I made for Adeline catches my eye over dinner, and I can't help but notice how much more she's smiling and talking. In fact, I can't remember the last time she talked so much during dinner.

While Adeline talks about New York City as if it's some truly magical place, Jax is practically beaming, looking completely enamored.

And I know exactly how he feels.

I know if I was capable of loving anyone, I could possibly love Adeline. She would be so easy to fall for.

Her fingers skim over the bracelet of the watch, and she looks up at me with a huge smile on her face. "Lucien gave me this today," she tells Jax, and she actually sounds…proud. Of the watch or of me or maybe both. I'm not sure.

But I can hear that forgotten muscle deep inside my chest beat once again under all the thick layers of tar and muck that have kept it hidden for so long.

Jax sends me an enigmatic look before he tells Adeline, "That was very thoughtful of him."

I'm sure he knows of my true intentions since he saw me installing some of the hardware in the watch the other day.

I built the watch almost entirely from scratch. It does a lot of the same tasks a fitness tracker does, except it's more advanced for my purposes. It contains a GPS tracker, and it's synced with my phone and computers so I know where she'll be at all times of the day.

The GPS will help us build a level of trust. It will alert me if her heartbeat reaches a certain level or if she strays too far away from the mansion. If she's trying to run, I will know almost instantly and be able to stop her.

I hope it never comes to that, but it's nice to know she'll never be able to leave me. If my security system and guards don't catch her, I can rely on the bracelet to do its job. The three-tier system should be foolproof.

* * * * * * *

AFTER DINNER, I retreat to the library with a glass of scotch. Adeline went up to her room to change into something, as she put it, more comfortable, but I expect her to be down shortly.

It feels weird to know she's roaming the halls of my mansion without a guard or me, and I can't help but check my phone for the tenth time in the past fifteen minutes to track her movements.

"She's in her room, right where she said she'd be," I mutter to myself.

I force myself to tuck my phone back into my pants pocket, and I take a sip of the dark liquid, relishing in the burn running down my throat.

I've never been much of a drinker, but I enjoy a good scotch now and then. I like to remain clearheaded and stay away from any substance that might be considered addictive. I know that all stems from my childhood and growing up with a drug-addicted whore of a mother who slept with anyone who supplied her with booze and pills. However, she had been devoid of reality for a long time, maybe even before I was born.

I was an unfortunate mistake.

My mother told me so. Many times.

I went through withdrawal from heroin soon after I was born. I spent an entire month in the NICU while I suffered from neonatal abstinence syndrome, or at least that's what my medical records tell me.

Memories from my childhood blur together. There are no happy memories, just nightmares that keep me up at night.

When I was finally rescued at the age of twelve by my rich uncle, many told him I was too far gone to be saved and that he should throw me into a mental institution.

I can't say I really blame them for their opinion of me, though. I mean, I barely spoke a word, couldn't make eye contact and had already developed a lot of nervous tics and social anxieties.

I was also extremely socially inept. Always assuming the worst in people. Always assuming they were going to hurt me even when they claimed to *love me*.

My mother had made sure to instill my fear of love right from birth. She had claimed to have loved me with all of her heart, but all she ever gave me was pain and misery.

I associated love with pain.

I still do.

My uncle must have had a heart of gold, though, because he never gave up on me. He spent money on the best doctors, the best therapists, eventually getting me to function like a normal human being at a rate so fast that it shocked all of my doctors.

I eventually grew into a *mostly* normal adult, and I learned to adapt to my surroundings quickly.

However, my peculiar mannerisms that I had developed over the years stuck with me, making me unable to pursue any sort of normal relationship with anyone really. My affinity to cleanliness came from living in scum my entire childhood. It soon grew to an obsession. And along with it, the need to feel clean and for everything around me to be sanitary.

I was only sixteen when my uncle noticed that I couldn't eat off the fine china that had already been used at a prior meal. I couldn't drink from the same glass that someone else's lips had touched even if it had been washed a million times in scalding hot water.

I needed everything to be brand new and unused. Every. Single. Time.

I also required control over every single aspect of my life. Having had no control for so long throughout my childhood, I demanded it when I got older. I need order and precision to survive.

Taking a final swig of my scotch, I set the glass down on a coaster resting on a side table. Feeling flushed from the alcohol and overwhelmed from the barrage of painful memories, I take off my suit jacket and neatly drape it over the back of a broad backed leather armchair. My fingers hook into the tie around my neck, loosening it, before unbuttoning the top two buttons.

Breathing deeply, I instantly feel better and not as if I'm suffocating.

The door to the library opens, and my gaze flashes to the doorway to see the most beautiful creature who ever graced my presence.

Adeline's dark locks cascade in soft waves around her. She's wearing short pajama shorts that showcase her long legs and curves and a tight tank that leaves no room for the imagination. She's not wearing a bra, and I can see her nipples poking through the material.

My cock jumps at the sight, straining against my zipper, and I hold back a groan as she walks towards me.

"I thought you might be in here," she says with a coy smile.

I try to read between the lines of her statement. She knew I'd be here, and she dressed…like *that*? I narrow my eyes as I try to figure out what kind of dangerous game she's trying to play.

"Jax told me that you don't even own a DVD player," she tells me.

I frown at her words, because I don't remember the two of them discussing that over dinner. She must have talked to him afterwards…or maybe before. How often do they talk? What do they talk about?

My mind swirls with jealously, and I hate the fucking feeling. I clench my jaw, seething internally with anger.

She must notice the change in my demeanor, because she takes a step back and watches me with a guarded look on her face. "You said that we could watch the *Lord of the Rings* movies together sometime, so I asked Jax if you had them."

Some of my raging jealousy simmers when I realize she was thinking about me when she talked to Jax.

Adeline regards me with unease, and I hate it. I don't want her to fear me or hate me. I want her to like me and to trust me, and I've never wanted something more in my entire fucking life.

I close the distance between us in a few, long strides. I tower over her petite frame as she looks up at me with those emerald eyes I can't seem to stop thinking about.

"I'll order a DVD player and the movies," I tell her. "If you make me a list, I'll get whatever movies you want."

She gives me a heart-stopping smile, and I can feel the breath leaving my lungs. Without thinking, I reach up and wrap a lock of her hair loosely around my finger. Her hair is soft, and I can smell the apple scent from the shampoo I bought for her.

"Lucien." My name is a soft plea on her lips.

When her pink tongue darts out of her mouth to lick her full lips, I'm a fucking goner. I curse at the scotch in my system right now giving me liquid courage and not a clear head. But maybe this is just what I need…what I want.

I release the strand and cup her cheek against my palm. Gently, I trace her bottom lip with the pad of my thumb. And suddenly, I feel the urge to do something I've never done before. My eyes lock onto her lips, and I lick my own. I want to kiss her. I want to taste her.

I want to fucking devour her.

She would be my first.

My first kiss…ever.

I suck in a shuddering breath, my entire body shaking with need.

"Adeline." I say her name, and it comes out almost like a moan. I don't ask if I can kiss her. I just take what I want. And I fucking want her more than anything in the world at this moment.

Leaning down, I brush my lips over hers in a teasing barely-there kiss. Softly at first, savoring the feeling of her mouth against mine for the first time.

My fingertips slowly trace the soft line of her jaw to the back of her neck. Then, I tangle my fingers into her hair and pull her closer, holding her in place as I deepen the kiss.

Adeline whimpers and opens willingly to me, welcoming me in as she parts her lips. My tongue slowly dips in, thrusting and intermingling with her own. She tastes like mint from her toothpaste, and I can't get enough of the taste. My hands hold her in place as I devour her, wanting more and more until I finally break away to take a ragged breath.

She's panting too, her eyes wide with surprise and confusion. She liked that kiss as much as I did even though she knows deep down that she shouldn't.

My lips are wet and warm from that soul-searing kiss, and I can still taste her on my tongue.

Slowly, dark thoughts begin to flood my mind about germs and who she might have kissed before and how dirty their mouths might have been…am I going to get sick from kissing her…what if she's sick right now…or has some kind of disease…

I squeeze my eyes shut and try to block out the unwanted thoughts.

Needing some distance, I take a step back from her, but Adeline follows me. "Lucien," she whispers, reaching for me, her delicate, soft hand cupping my cheek.

But her touch is too much on my senses, which are already overloaded from that kiss; and I take another step back to break our connection. My entire body trembles, and I feel like I can't get enough air into my lungs.

Without saying another word, I grab my suit jacket and rush out the door, leaving Adeline standing there. Alone and confused.

CHAPTER 31

LUCIEN

(ONE WEEK LATER)

I TAKE A break from working and walk over to the large windows in my office overlooking the property. Grabbing a pair of binoculars from the windowsill, I peer into them.

Off in the distance, Adeline sits in the butterfly garden I had planted for her, reading. Her nose is always stuck in a book, and it's one of the many things I can't help but love about her.

I've been allowing her to explore the grounds near the mansion, and so far she hasn't broken any of my rules or my trust. Not even once.

I find myself longing for her smile constantly, longing for her affection. And I haven't been able to deny her a single thing she asks for.

Except for freedom, that is.

After our first kiss in the library and my anxiety-riddled brain went on overload mode, I've been taking things slow with Adeline, one day at a time. I haven't been able to kiss her again, but I'm determined to feel her sweet, soft lips against mine again soon.

I can feel the smile on my face as I watch Adeline through the binoculars. She's the most beautiful creature I've ever seen, and I find myself a lot of times just observing her. She has turned my whole world upside down, and I can't even fathom the possibility of losing her now.

I've been keeping track of the Valenti family's whereabouts, comings and goings but, most importantly, that of Giovanni Morello's.

Word finally spread just the other day in the dark underground of New York that Salvatore Valenti's youngest daughter is missing and presumed kidnapped…or dead.

They have no idea where Adeline is, and I intend on keeping it that way.

If I was a betting man, I would have bet all my fortune on the fact that Valenti would have murdered his right-hand man the moment he came back from his trip to California and found his daughter missing.

And yet Giovanni still has a pulse.

Perhaps there is more to the story than what I understand. Maybe Valenti has no idea that Giovanni is behind his daughter's disappearance. And maybe he has no idea as to the lengths that Giovanni would go to make some fast cash.

Regardless, Giovanni continues to live, and I continue to keep his former fiancée here.

And I'm not planning on letting her go.

CHAPTER 32

GIOVANNI

"WHERE IS SHE?!" Salvatore Valenti practically screams as he slams his fist down on his large, oak desk. The wood threatens to splinter under the assault, and I hurry to swallow past the lump lodged in my throat.

After a week of giving the mafia king the runaround on the whereabouts of his daughter when he returned from a longer than expected trip to California, he finally called me in for a meeting. And I don't mean with a courtesy call. I'm still feeling the bumps and bruises from being manhandled and thrown into the back of a black SUV in the middle of the night.

So here I am, sitting in a leather chair in the center of Sal's office, wearing a crumpled white t-shirt and black, cotton lounge pants after being rudely awakened by the sound of thugs breaking into my condo. They searched the whole place before we left, no doubt per their boss's orders, and came up empty, of course.

Adeline wasn't there. Adeline isn't even in the United States, as far as I'm aware. *The Wolf* has her.

And instead of returning her, as agreed upon, he's *keeping her*. And I am so fuckin' fucked.

Swallowing hard again, I manage to tell Salvatore, "Adeline was kidnapped a few weeks ago while you were in Cali." I don't dare tell him that she was kidnapped the night he left or the fact that I paid off her bodyguards to keep their traps shut.

I managed to keep Bruno and Dario in the dark over the past several weeks, feeding them lies about Adeline's whereabouts. They thought she was safe and sound with me, and they enjoyed spending the fuck out of my hush money whilst not having to babysit.

However, they paid the price dearly when Salvatore returned home and the two of them couldn't answer his questions as to why Adeline wasn't in her room safe and sound. Sal didn't waste any time showing them what he thought of their negligence.

He slit their fuckin' throats.

But I have earned something over the years that Bruno and Dario never did --- Salvatore's trust. Sal trusts me not to lie to him. He trusts me not to fuck up. And he trusts me so much that he's willing to welcome me into his family by allowing me to marry his daughter and produce an heir to take over the entire empire someday.

"So, she's been missing for weeks, and I'm just now finding out the truth," he states matter-of-factly.

I can practically hear the blood start to boil in Salvatore's veins. He calmly stands, his hands clenching into fists at his sides, the only indication that he's losing his cool. If there's one thing I know about Salvatore, it's that he's always the three Cs --- cool, calm and collected. Even when he's a raging lunatic or on a killing spree, he always seems like he knows exactly what he's doing in the heat of the moment. He never wavers past the point of no return. He's always present, in the moment, doing the task at hand.

"I trusted you." He spits the words out as if they're full of venom. "I trusted you with my youngest daughter."

I hang my head in shame. This wasn't supposed to happen. I was thinking solely about the money, all the fuckin' money. And now I've lost the most important thing in my life. Did I love Adeline? No. I loved what she could give me. She gave me the chance to be second in command to the most powerful mafia boss on the east coast. I knew without a doubt that once we were married, Salvatore would consider me his *son*. And with that title, I would assume new responsibilities. I would have the life most men in my world only dream about.

"I knew how important your business was in Cali, and so I tried to find her, tried to get her back on my own without causing a ripple in the pond."

"Oh, you didn't create a ripple, Giovanni. You created a fucking tidal wave." He slowly rolls the sleeves of his black shirt over his thick, hairy forearms. "Tell me everything you know," Salvatore says in a calm voice that causes a chill to run up my spine.

I recount the story back to him of the kidnapping, not giving him any more details than necessary and making it seem like an ordinary mugging in the city with nothing to link her disappearance back to me. I exaggerate about the amount of men, however, knowing that he won't believe that I couldn't overcome just a few men.

"Those fucks took my daughter," he says through clenched teeth with rage practically sprouting out of every greasy pore in his body.

"I tried finding her on my own. I should have told you right away, Boss. I'm sorry," I tell him hurriedly, sweat beginning to drip down my temples. My life is starting to flash before my eyes. I've seen a guy get gutted for a hell of a lot less in this very room.

"You kept this from me," Salvatore says, seething, while he slowly stands and rounds the desk. His pudgy hand shoots out and grabs me by my collar, pulling tight and strangling me in the process. "You shouldn't have done that. I control this fucking city. I could have found her in less than an hour," he spits, saliva running down my cheek. "I should kill you just for being such a stupid *fuck*," he snarls, wringing my neck back and forth roughly for several seconds before finally releasing his hold on me. "But you're engaged to my daughter, and that is the *only* reason you're alive right now. Don't you fucking forget it," he warns me, pointing his finger at me.

I nod vehemently, choking to get air back into my lungs after his assault. "Yes, Boss. We'll find her. We're going to get her back," I tell him, not knowing if I'm trying to convince him or myself.

"You're goddamn right we're going to get her back." He grabs his cell phone off of his desk and presses a few buttons. After a muffled voice speaks on the other end, he says, "Adeline was kidnapped. I need all manpower on this. And when you find the *fucks* that are responsible, don't kill them. I want all of their pain and blood on my hands."

I swallow hard at his words. If Salvatore finds out I'm the one behind Adeline's disappearance, it won't matter that I'm her fiancé or that he trusted me. He'll fucking kill me…but not until after he makes me suffer through a long, torturous and painful revenge.

I put my head in my hands, visibly distraught and not knowing how the fuck to fix this. When Salvatore clasps his hand on my shoulder, I nearly jump out of my chair.

"Don't worry," he says to me in a calmer voice, obviously thinking I'm upset about Adeline's disappearance and not shitting myself over the fact that I'm terrified of him and what he'll do to me if he finds out the truth. "We'll find her," he tells me with all the confidence in the world.

I hope he's right. I've tried finding her for weeks with no more information than when I started. Adeline disappeared off the face of the earth when I sold her. And if her father ever finds out what I did, it will be the end of me and everything I've worked so hard for.

I rub my blurry eyes, tired and bloodshot from lack of sleep. I haven't slept more than a few minutes since she was kidnapped. I worry constantly about whether she's eating or sleeping or being tortured. If I don't get her back safe and sound, my life as I knew it is fuckin' over.

My decision to sell her was so extraordinarily stupid that I still can't believe it's real. I feel like I'm in a never-ending nightmare that I can't wake myself out of.

I did this. It's all my fault. And if the truth were to ever come out…then I'm a dead man walking.

CHAPTER 33

ADELINE

IT'S A SUNNY, breezy morning when I venture outside to the butterfly garden that Lucien had planted for me a couple of weeks ago. It still feels weird to leave the house or even my room on my own without someone in tow or someone watching.

I sit down amongst the beautiful flowers and watch the numerous swallowtails and monarchs flutter around me. This is my favorite place to go to read and just be by myself. It's on the edge of the property, away from prying eyes, although I don't doubt that there are cameras in place somewhere around me.

I decide I don't care, however. In the past few weeks, I've become accustomed to this island and to everyone who inhabits it…especially Lucien.

Call me crazy, but there have been some serious moments of chemistry between us. I just can't make heads or tails of the whole thing, however.

One moment I want him. The next I want nothing to do with him.

I play the *what if* game a million times in my head every day.

What if Gio found me? Would I go back with him?

What if I stay here on the island? What would happen between Lucien and me? Could we truly ever be happy?

I have a million questions with no answers in sight. And I suppose only time will tell what will really happen to me...to Luc...to us, if there even is an *us*.

Sometimes it feels like he doesn't want to even be in the same room as me, and other times I feel his obsession and need for me like a magnetic pull drawing me in.

Lucien is an enigma, and that's putting it extremely lightly. I don't even think his own cousin understands him. When Lucien goes off the deep end, Jax will just shrug and say, "Leave him alone until he works out whatever the hell he needs worked out."

Luc has a past that I've only caught a glimpse of hidden in his deep dark gaze. I'd love to uncover it, bury myself inside his brain until I could learn every little secret he keeps so tightly guarded.

Jax told me before that Luc had a terrible childhood, but that it was his story to tell.

What if Lucien never tells me? What if we go through our lives on this island and I never get to know the real Lucien?

Sighing, I tuck my hair behind my ear and bend down to breathe in the scent of the tropical flower in full bloom. Maria told me it's some type of lily, but I can't remember the name of it. All I know is that it's beautiful and smells like heaven.

Maybe I'll ask Lucien to order me some books about flowers and how to identify them. He already bought me one about birds, and I devoured it, wanting to know every kind of fowl feathered friend I've been religiously feeding for weeks.

I didn't think many birds would be on an island, but they must have migrated here at some point. And some are so beautiful and bright that they take my breath away.

Plucking the lily from the ground, I shove the stem behind my ear to hold it in place. I do this often, wanting the scent of the beautiful flowers around me constantly.

Then I stand up, dusting the grass and dirt from my denim capris. It's almost lunchtime, according to the watch that Lucien gave me. And as if right on cue, my stomach growls loudly.

Maria makes the most spectacular meals, and I've been hitting up Luc's private gym even harder to make up for all the extra calories. I work out a few times a week, sometimes even alongside Luc.

I grin when I think of his nickname that I've been calling him. Luc fits him. And more often than not lately, he's been easier to deal with, more casual and…happier than I've ever seen him.

I'd like to think I play a part in that, but who knows. It's not like *he* would ever tell me.

On my way back to the mansion, I cut through the small orchard with the hopes of snagging some fruit on the way when I'm stopped by the gardener, who I've become familiar with. He's short with bronzed skin, dark eyes and a thick accent. He's always friendly, but there's something about him that rubs me the wrong way. I can't put my finger on it, but sometimes I catch him staring at me with an expression that I can't quite decipher, and it gives me the creeps.

"Hi, Rafael," I call to him, giving him a wave.

Rafael's eyes dart around before he puts his finger to his lips to shush me. My mouth instantly snaps shut. As he steps closer to me, his dark eyes study me closely. "You want go home?" he asks in broken English.

My gaze snaps to his, searching his face for any ulterior motives. He can get me off of this island? The *what if* game has suddenly become a very real possibility. Maybe if I could get back home and tell my father what happened, he could protect me. Then there would be no reason for Luc to take on that responsibility of keeping me safe.

"Y-yes," I stammer. "I do. Please. Can you help me leave?"

He nods and motions for me to follow him. My eyes dart back to the mansion, and I suddenly get a sinking feeling in the pit of my stomach. In my excitement to leave and get back to my old life, I didn't take the time to consider everything I'd be leaving behind...and *who* I'd be leaving behind.

But I refuse to be held prisoner for the rest of my life with an uncertain future. Lucien holds all the power here. Maybe once I'm back home he could visit me, and we could go from there....if he even still wants me by then.

I tear my eyes away from the mansion and reluctantly follow the man. Even though he gives me the creeps, maybe he's a nice guy on the inside. If he's willing to help me, he must have a good heart. No one else has been willing to go against their *master*.

The man begins to jog, motioning with his hand for me to hurry up. I begin to run behind him, my short legs trying to match his long strides.

He leads me farther and farther away from the security of the grounds, and I'm suddenly feeling uneasy. I realize in that moment how safe Lucien makes me feel. Even though he's my captor, he's so protective over me. He would never let anything bad happen to me.

A lump lodges in my throat as I finally push my escape plans aside and begin to think about the consequences of my actions. I don't even know Rafael other than the fact that he works for Lucien.

What if he's not even planning to take me home? And what happens if I do get home? Will my father ever let me out of his sight again? Will Gio even want me anymore after he finds out what happened? If he doesn't...then my life will return to what it was before...filled with abuse and me being my father's little puppet.

And there is no way my father would ever let me contact Lucien. Besides, it's not like I have Luc's address or phone number.

I'll never see him again.

That thought causes me to stop dead in my tracks, and Rafael looks back at me with confusion lacing his dark features.

"Wait. I can't do this. I want to go back," I say in a panic. I'd wanted to leave this island so badly for so long that my natural instincts had been overshadowed, but now I'm starting to think clearly. I wanted to leave before...before I started falling for my captor.

I take a step back, and suddenly Rafael's whole demeanor changes.

His face crumples in anger, and he stares at me through narrow slits as he stalks towards me. He's not my savior after all. He's just another monster living in the shadows of this island.

I turn to run, but I only make it a few feet before he tackles me to the ground. I struggle against him as best I can, but he quickly overpowers me. He hauls me up by my hair, and his large hand clamps down on my mouth before I can scream.

I kick and thrash with all my might, my sneakers kicking up plumes of dust and dirt until my left one eventually comes off, as he half pulls, half drags me towards a row of small cottages up ahead.

Knowing what he's planning on doing, I fight even harder, but my efforts soon prove to be futile. I would have better luck wrestling a grizzly bear. Instead, I scream and scream until my voice is hoarse.

The man pulls me inside of the cottage and throws me on a dirty mattress on the floor that smells like moldy cheese and other things I can't even fathom. Bile rises up in my throat, and I gag.

I glance to the right and left of me trying to find a weapon, but coming up empty considering the Spartan furnishings of the small room.

The man menacingly steps towards me, but I hold my hands out and scream at him, "Stop! Please! Let me go!"

He tackles me onto the mattress, and I struggle under him, trying to escape. The only thought in my head is that I need Luc. Above everything, he would protect me. He would never allow this to happen.

And so I begin to scream my dark angel's name over and over and over again as loud as I can.

"Shut up!" the man hisses at me before wrapping his hands around my throat.

Lucien's name dies in my throat as Rafael squeezes so tightly that I can't pull air into my lungs. Black dots form in my vision, but I refuse to allow the darkness to take over. If I pass out, then I can't fight back…and then he can do *anything* he wants.

I buck under him, using the last of my strength to kick up my knee. The first strike gets him in the gut, but the second is a bullseye, and I land my knee right into his balls.

Rafael roars in pain and lets me go, and I scramble back away from him. He's hurt, but not incapacitated and will quickly recover. Thinking fast, I dart for the front door, but he snags my ankle on the way. I fall forward quickly, but am able to brace myself at the last second before I face plant on the hard floor.

My attacker twists my leg, turning me over onto my back, and comes down hard with his thighs on either side of my waist. With a growl, he grabs a fistful of my hair and slams my head back on the unforgiving concrete floor, jarring my skull. A ringing sensation is in my ears as I try to find my bearings. I'm dazed from the hard hit, and I can feel a searing pain in the back of my head.

Rafael gets up, easily taking me with him and throws me down on the mattress once more. The room spins around me as I fall back, unable to stay upright.

"Lucien!" I plead, begging for him to hear me, but knowing he won't.

He's not coming for me.

And I don't know if I can survive this.

To be continued...

ABOUT THE AUTHOR

Thank you for reading! If you enjoyed reading Keeping Her, please consider telling your friends and posting a short review on Amazon. Word of mouth is an author's best friend and much appreciated. Shouts from rooftops are great too.

Adeline and Lucien's story continues in Saving Him, the next book in the Keep Me Series.

Saving Him will be released on 9/23/17.

Pre-order your copy on Amazon.

You can find all of my books exclusively on Amazon and free for Kindle Unlimited subscribers: http://amazon.com/author/angelasnyder

And please sign up for my newsletter to be notified of all of my new releases, giveaways, sneak peeks, freebies and more: http://eepurl.com/cNF0o5

Made in United States
Cleveland, OH
05 February 2025

14056767R00111